good deed rain

Credits:

Cover, design and illustration: © Fred Sodt

Dandelion chapter drawing and writing: Allen Frost

Apple by TFK!

From the beginning, thank you to Robert Bussard for sharing his grandmother's elephant story. For research help, my thanks go out to my friend, Eric Mastor and The Center for Pacific Northwest Studies, also to Jeff Jewell at The Whatcom Museum and *The Bellingham Herald* whose microfilm reel time-machined me right back into July, 1942. Finally, I wish to thank Fred Sodt who brought the words magically to life.

If you have enjoyed this book
please share it with someone

ALLEN FROST

ILLUSTRATIONS BY
FRED SODT

I DREAMED I WROTE a book named Roosevelt. I put that title in my notebook and carried it around for a while and then I remembered a story that Robert told me. Sometime at the turn of the 20th century, a circus came to Bellingham and the elephant escaped. Robert's grandmother, who was a young girl at the time, loved to tell the story of how the elephant lived in Whatcom Creek. Somehow that story found the title *Roosevelt* and once linked, began to gain speed and steamed over the spring months from March to May 2014, creating this book. Although I played with history, time and place, enough of this 1942 world really happened. There was a fairground where the circus would come every summer, "Bringing Joy and Cheer to a Troubled World," and I wanted to write about the war. The war that hasn't stopped. I remember listening to my grandparents tell me stories of that time. My grandfather had seen his share of it. He even met the German U-Boat captain who had sunk his ship. When he told me about that, he always made it a point that I understood clearly, the enemy he had seen was no different than us. And as my grandmother listened she would always chime in, "Really and truly." Finally, I've always wanted to write one of those old paperback Scholastic Books...with a map you could follow as you read and with drawings along the way. I remember how thrilling it was in gradeschool when we would get those Scholastic book order forms, pencil in the titles you want, bring in dollars from home in an envelope, and then one afternoon later on, the teacher would open up a box. After all those years, now here it is...Roosevelt.

Allen Frost
May 26, 2014
Bellingham, Washington

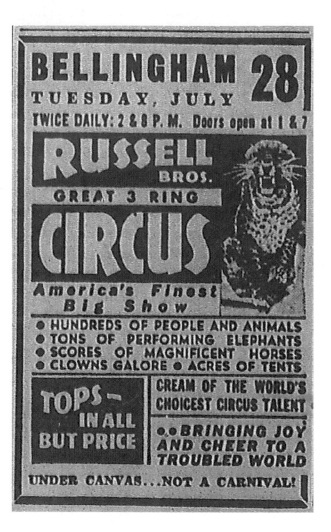

BELLINGHAM 28
TUESDAY, JULY
TWICE DAILY: 2 & 8 P. M. Doors open at 1 & 7

RUSSELL
BROS.
GREAT 3 RING
CIRCUS
America's Finest
Big Show

● HUNDREDS OF PEOPLE AND ANIMALS
● TONS OF PERFORMING ELEPHANTS
● SCORES OF MAGNIFICENT HORSES
● CLOWNS GALORE ● ACRES OF TENTS

TOPS —
IN ALL
BUT PRICE

CREAM OF THE WORLD'S
CHOICEST CIRCUS TALENT

●●BRINGING JOY
AND CHEER TO A
TROUBLED WORLD

UNDER CANVAS...NOT A CARNIVAL!

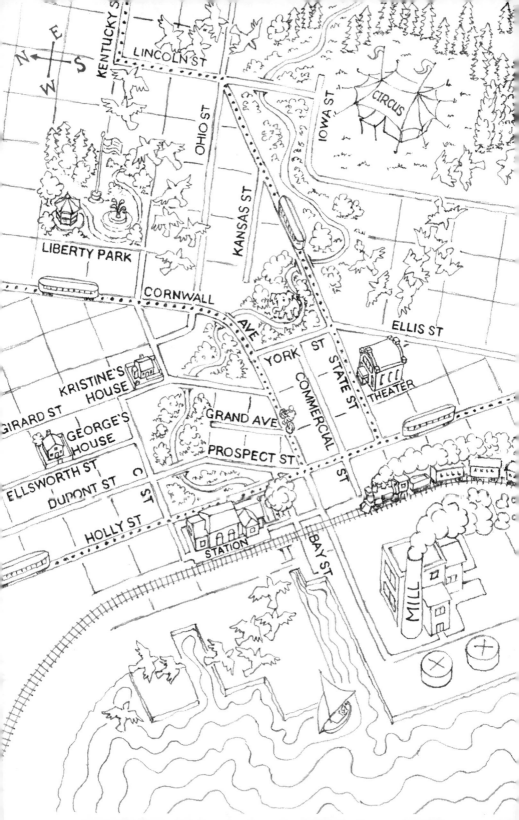

The clicking clacking of the railroad tracks sewed up the night. With the wind and passing land, the long blur went by the little towns and fields and shook back into the trees. Coal black smoke from the engine hid its brightly painted wooden cars, blanketed the rumble of all its metal wheels, the singing of its creaks and whistling speed. Far down the line where the tracks bent and slowed towards the sea, the telegraph clicked, dots and dashes, station to station. Along the way, the word was passed on…The circus train was coming.

The first person to know about the train was Robert Canfield. He was in the little room translating the telegraph while the station agent made coffee in a blue metal urn.

Robert was so excited to tell his nephew that he almost ran from the shack, through the railyard and onto Holly Street. Like the street lamps of shining pearls strung through the quiet dawn, Robert knew the news would go like wildfire from block to block.

He turned on C Street. It was nearly empty. It was summertime and not much reason for anyone to get up this early. He saw the milk truck and Bill with his basket full of bottles but he didn't want to stop and talk. He was in a hurry to George.

In one hand, Robert carried a black metal lunchbox, his other hand held an empty thermos. Actually, it rattled from the lemon rinds he put in with his tea. The night was seeping away, leaving a violet sky clear of cloud just before the sky would brighten into soft blue and pink. Later it would be a beautiful July day. To the east, the sun was starting the town slow. The factory blew its plume west, towards the Japanese Empire.

Along the nearby creek, the thick canopy of chestnut trees let him walk in a dark and cool midnight.

The early morning air was filled with calling birds. He passed picket fences and the one house with a light on. It was a little blue house set back from the sidewalk, across a lawn where grass and weedy flowers grew tall. An orange light shone in what Robert guessed was the kitchen. As he walked by, Robert didn't see anyone in there, but he heard a record playing jazz orchestra. That was Cornelius Barter's house. That boy lived and breathed jazz. He was in there sitting down and listening with his trumpet, his fingers moving to the song, longing to get older so he could really play.

The street got quieter as Robert walked along but he still thought about Cornelius. He was older than George by a few years. One time, on a morning like this, Cornelius was sitting in the yard with his trumpet. Robert asked him if he was okay, and the boy told him, "I'm practicing staying up all night." That's what his idols all did. Robert wondered what the boy's parents thought, but he never did see any sign of them. For all he knew, Cornelius lived in that run-down house all alone with his trumpet and records, waiting to be old enough to leave.

The lemons in his thermos clunked about as Robert shifted his lunchbox to the other hand. He was nearly to George's house. Every summer the circus came to town and ever since school let out, the boy had been asking Robert if he had any news. What he didn't want to tell his nephew was something else he

11

heard. Maybe it was a rumor, but because of the war, this might be the circus' last visit to town. You couldn't have a circus with all its wild animals and magical performers crisscrossing about a nation at war. Robert knew the war was only beginning to take its toll.

He turned on the corner of Ellsworth. There was another house with a light inside. Some people were starting to get up for work. He knew the man in that house. He worked at the *Herald*. He would be reading the stories that came off the wire, stories of ships and airplanes and cities in flame in a war that was far away. Back at the station, during all those slow hours, Robert liked to read the *Herald*. Past the front page though, he skipped to see what movies were playing that day.

Oh…he breathed deeply. There were flowers on this street. His feet slowed, he hovered at the wooden gate of the yard where so many different flowers bunched and bloomed. He even sighed. It was amazing. After an evening at the station where the coal dust picked up and mixed with the factory pulp and where the smell of the sea could only rarely get through to clean, this yard was enough to turn him into a bumbling bee. He took another deep breath to fill himself up with the scent of flowers before he left. Only another block to go…

A robin shot by him, followed by another so fast he thought they were bats. They squabbled over the territory of lawns and branches.

Sometimes he kept going down to F Street where

there was a café on the corner. He could see the green-ish yellow glow of its windows. Maybe Bill was in there now with his basket of milk bottles, with a stack of his Socialist newspapers left by the door.

Robert passed the telephone pole covered with runners of blackberry climbing it almost up to the electric wires. Now he could see the house and George's window. Of course it was still dark and shel-tered by the leaves of an alder.

A train moved somewhere along the harbor. He heard a dog barking a block away as he left the side-walk and onto the grass.

There was a big Victory Garden for him to walk around. George's mother, Robert's sister, had tied up the peas in tall ship masts. He passed their harbor and approached George's window. A small blue sailboat lay on its side beneath the glass. George used it to climb inside his room, though his brother Andrew kept say-ing he would make it seaworthy again.

Robert brushed against the waist high sunflowers that stood along this side of the house, then rested his elbows on the sill. The window was pushed open. Rob-ert touched the checkered curtain and looked inside.

His nephew's bedroom was a blue wool sweater, still as a pool of water, though he could see the dim outline of the dresser, the bed and the circus posters tacked to the wall. On a table sat the boy's shortwave radio with the wooden microphone tied to it by a string. Sometimes at night, George told him, he would tune into the world, the Armed Forces radio, Berlin, Rome and Tokyo and tell them to stop fighting. Even though, George knew, those places could never hear his voice connected to a radio by twine and some pieces of hammered wood.

Robert pursed his lips and made the call of a chickadee. That high pitched sound flew into the dawn room, followed by another and soon by the third time, the boy stirred.

George sat up and looked at his window. "Uncle Robert?" he said. He rubbed the sleep off his eyes. "What day is it?"

Robert smiled. "July 24, 1942..." He drummed his fingers on the windowsill, dots and dashes that were the language of the telegraph. He slowed the code down. It was one word. Like the sound of the chickadee, he had taught it to George, and he repeated it until from the look on the boy's face he knew that George understood. Robert laughed when the boy almost shouted, "Circus!"

That was Robert's message delivered, and he left, but early as it was, George couldn't fall back asleep. For a long while he lay in bed, watching his room. He studied the airplane suspended on a thread from the ceiling, watched its very slow movement. And he saw how the sun began to change the room from dark to a sort of movie house glow that became bright enough to read the book titles on the shelf next to his bed.

They were an easy reach away and so finally he stretched out an arm to get one. He ran his fingers over the book's embossed cover. An elephant held a clown, juggling high above the ground. George had a whole section of those circus books—he could read himself into the circus anytime he wanted, but this was the actual day their train was arriving in his town. He put the book back. He couldn't sit still.

George pulled his bathrobe off the end of his bed and put it on. He tied the belt and couldn't resist becoming Houdini, pinning his hands under the cloth and then breaking the chain of that soft knot and freeing himself. He held up his hands to the imaginary applause.

He heard the bicycle of the paperboy as it squeaked past their house. He listened hard but didn't hear the newspaper land. The boy hardly ever hit their step. It was probably on their lawn. George's father hated that. He would have to read around the dew.

Quickly fastening his robe again, George left his room. There wasn't much time to save the *Herald* from drowning in the damp leaves of grass and dandelions.

In the hall outside his room, George faced his brother's door. The hush from in there was palpable. Andrew had been served his draft notice yesterday. Soon a train would be coming for him, like the one George had seen a few mornings ago, when he stopped his bicycle to watch. The slow rumble shook the ground as the troop train passed through town—bells ringing, red lights, thunder on the trestles…All the faces looking out.

George padded quietly down the hallway. His parents' door was still shut too but he knew they would be getting up soon. His father had to go to work. Out in the living room he could hear the ticking of the big wooden clock on the mantle. A circus book was where he left it on the red chair by the radio. Last night they listened to *The Thin Man* before bed.

He crossed the room and turned the gold handle of the front door.

Birds were singing. Little ones were in all the branches while three robins scouted across the lawn, heads cocked, listening for worms. Those three birds took to wing as George stepped off the doorstep onto the wet grass.

The newspaper was sitting in a plush collapse

of the tall grass. That reminded him that his father wanted George to use the mower today. If he did it right after breakfast, he could go straight to the station afterwards. He was not going to miss that circus train pulling in.

George dodged a bee, early on its way to catch the first waking flowers. He picked up the *Herald* and was glad it wasn't too wet. The paper was rolled and tied with a string. As he fumbled with the loose knot, George thought about that person who would have to twine all those *Heralds* tight, morning after morning.

At the front door he got the string off and dropped the squiggle of it into his bathrobe pocket. He actually supposed there was a chance the circus would be on the front page. It wasn't though—it was always the war.

Nazis Slash Deep Into Red Line.

Well, maybe there would be something about the circus further on…George opened the door.

The kitchen light was on. His mother appeared in the frame, holding a mixing bowl. "George! Are you walking in your sleep?" she smiled.

He held up the newspaper and carried it into the kitchen. The heater was on; warm air blew across the tiles over his bare feet. He sat down at the small table and spread the paper across its Formica top.

The kitchen was brought to life. His mother was busy stirring. The coffee pot began to percolate rhythmically. A radio on the counter next to her was softly playing the morning show, *Breakfast Symphony*.

"Uncle Robert woke me up this morning."

"He did?"

George yawned. "Yeah. He heard on the telegraph the circus is coming today."

"Oh boy!" His mother poured some pancake batter onto the hot frying pan. It sizzled, sending out a smell that made George lick his lips.

"I suppose you'll be down at the station waiting for it?"

George coughed. He had been riding on the smell of those pancakes like a magic carpet. "Mmhmm," he agreed. The newspaper crackled beneath his hands as he spread it open on the table. He quickly turned past that front page.

Of course he was looking for circus news. For the past week there had been premonitions, tantalizing hints that the circus was on the way. The Saturn Circus! A picture of a woman on an elephant…A trained seal…A clown…Little ads at the bottom of page 5 or 6. He would cut them out and glue them in the notebook he kept in his desk.

But there on the second page of the *Herald*, George was stopped by something else instead. He read the bold letters out loud to his mother, "Married Men Last in Draft…Husbands will be the last ones called. Boards directed to call single men first."

Then he was stopped as his mother put her hand down over the story. "I hate this war," she said. She

18

cupped her other hand tight around George's slim shoulder.

He felt the sigh leave her. It took form in the air, quiet and frozen as his brother's shut door. There didn't seem to be any way out of the war, he thought, even as his mother bent and kissed the top of his head.

"Hey!"

They both jumped.

"Who's burning the chow?" George's father peeled the smoking pancakes off the hot skillet. He set the blackened circles on a plate as his wife hurried over.

"Oh…" she said. She rubbed at her eyes with the back of her hand.

"It's alright," he said. "I like my pancakes well done." He moved the plate away to give her room and he kissed her wet cheek.

"You hungry, George?" she asked.

George turned the newspaper page. "You bet I am! Dad, the circus is coming today! Uncle Robert heard it on the telegraph. Here look—it's in the paper!" He put his finger on the story and read.

"One night only. The Saturn Circus. Three rings full of wonder. A performing menagerie of elephants, horses, seals, tigers and lions. Featuring, magic, aerial acrobatics and unsurpassed entertainment. Bringing joy and cheer to a troubled world."

George's father sat at the small table with him and listened. After a bite of the pancake he decided the best way to eat it was give each crunching forkful a dip in his hot coffee. That softened it a little. "What time did Uncle Robert say the circus train will arrive?" he asked as George reached the end of his news.

George looked up from the page. "Gee, he didn't say..."

"He forgot to mention that?" George's father gave his wife a look, a roll of the eyes that George had seen before when Uncle Robert's name came up. It was like a routine in a movie.

She shot her husband a look back. "The important thing is it's happening today and Uncle Robert was kind enough to let George know."

Her husband was going to say something else about her brother, but his pancake fell off into his coffee mug. "Aah!" he cried. He fished at the broken scorch with his fork.

"There you are," she told him then she turned back to the stove and prepared a plateful of only slightly blackened pancakes for her son.

George pushed the *Herald* across to his father. As his mother approached, George patted his flannel covered belly. "Thanks, Mom. I'm so hungry I could eat a horse. Correction...An elephant."

"Well, you have to save some for your brother."

George groaned and poured maple syrup.

George's father looked up from the newspaper. "Where *is* Andrew? Still asleep?"

"Let him sleep." She moved the griddle off the burner. "At least I know where he is and he's safe and sound. He's in our house not on some troop ship or—"

Her husband sighed. He couldn't look at that front page either. He stood up and carried his plate to the sink. He tried to say something to her, "I…" but all he could do was put his arms around her.

George thought it was almost funny, with the orchestra music on the radio they could almost be dancing. But George saw she still held the wooden spoon, almost touching her father's fine blue shirt uniform. One time, when she heard George say 'Damn,' she had chased him around the kitchen with that spoon. Now it was a sad spoon, like a wooden flower that lost its petals.

About an hour later George was twenty feet off the ground. Up in the thick canopy of leaves he stared down past his green, grass-stained shoes to the station platform below.

He had raced here after cutting the lawn, the whole time listening past the chattering of the mower blades for the train he didn't dare miss. He knew he left a few uneven tracks of grass and clover but he had to hurry. When he was done, he grabbed his bicycle from the shed and rode like lightning across the blocks and alleys down to the bay. Once in the station he asked, but nobody seemed to know exactly when the circus train would arrive. He just had to wait for it to happen. He chose the tall chestnut tree near the platform. He could climb it and see far down the tracks, across to where the rails turned at the factory. When it did arrive, he would be the first to see the black smoke and hear the steam-chuffing squeal of its metal wheels. He was prepared to watch for it all day.

This was a good tree too. Close as it was to the station, nobody noticed him. How many people hurrying about ever look up into trees? There could be all kinds of kids hiding in them, watching. George loved being up in a tree. He couldn't see the appeal of joining in the grownup rush. It was summer, he was done with fourth grade and he felt like he had all the time in the world.

He even had a book with him. He brought it with a sandwich from home. Unlatching the leather bag hooked to a branch nearby, George reached in and took out a thick Big Little Book, *Charlie Chan at the Circus*. His parents, the lady at the library, his brother and teachers all told him he could read other things than circus books—there were hundreds of great books that didn't have big tops, trained animals and clowns. "That's okay," he would say. He knew what he liked.

He read his book. In his hands, the newsprint pages became a separate reality. The one existing outside of the tree radioed its presence in the background. The sound of town was only a song to read by.

The book was getting good. The elephant was delivering secret messages, the trapeze girl was in danger, there was a magician following Charlie Chan between the dark tents. George was startled when he heard a familiar silver bell. It was like an alarm clock waking up a dream.

"Hey, George!"

Kristine was stopped on her bicycle below him. She held her hand up to shade her eyes. Her orange hair sparkled in the sunshine. "What are you doing?"

"I'm waiting for the circus train."

She laughed. "In a tree?"

"I get a good view this way. You want to come up?"

"I guess so." She parked her bicycle next to his, leaned against the tree trunk.

"There's a good hand-hold on this side…" George pointed. He put his book back in the hanging bag and watched her climb.

"How long have you been up here?" she asked as she settled herself on the branch.

"I guess an hour or so."

"It's nice. When do you think the circus is getting here?"

"I'm not sure. A couple freight trains came through earlier. Hey, you want some of my sandwich?"

"Sure."

He broke her off a piece and passed it.

"Thanks." She took a bite and a moment to look around.

George watched her eat. He saw a tiny green aphid on her bare freckled arm and he liked the way she noticed it too and put her fingertip near it, and let it climb on so she could give it a big leaf to live on. Be kind to animals, no matter how little or big.

"You're like Tarzan up here," she told him.

"Me, Tarzan," he said. "You, Jane."

And from far away they heard a shrill whistle curl in the air.

A flock of birds, starlings and some crows that they didn't know were there took off from the crown of their tree.

Kristine lost George for a moment in the train hissing steam, the thunder of pounding trestles, bells and that shrieking whistle. "George!" she shouted and grabbed at his shirt sleeve.

"Come on!" he grinned back at her.

The platform was crowded with people now, drawn magnetically to the circus train.

"Look!" George cried.

Past the black chuffing engine car clouding up the sky with black cloud and the hot volcano breath of a dragon, behind the tender, was a boxcar with red flags on top. Along its wooden sides in painted big letters read the words, SATURN CIRCUS.

"It's them! It's them!" George shouted.

The train gave another dying scream and its screeching wheels stopped the long line of cars with a jolt.

They heard doors opening. Further down the track was a passenger car and George pulled Kristine along, dodging the growing crowd. Kristine squeezed his arm tight as a band started to play, brass horns and clarinets and a bass drum booming.

"This way!" George yelled. They scurried between some soldiers and stopped with a view, right on the edge of the platform where they could see all the way down the train to the end.

"Jeepers!" Kristine said in his ear as a man in a tuxedo stepped outside, right onto a pair of stilts and suddenly became ten feet tall, waving above the crowd. And he was only the beginning. After him the circus avalanched out.

George and Kristine moved in the crowd as it bumped and streamed with wooden carts stacked high with bags and steamer trunks, mixed in with performers and people like them looking and jostling, laughing and pointing.

Some railway men set up a roped off barricade, and George took Kristine close to the line so they could watch the unloading. Inside those boxcars in cages and stalls were all the animals.

Ramps were pulled to hauled-open doors, as men hurried over tarps untying knots; there was all kinds of noise and dazzling commotion.

They watched more performers leave the train— whole families, a man spinning his top hat on a cane with a monkey grinning from his shoulder, clowns dressed in bright checkered suits, a woman with a genuine parasol.

All along the train the circus was piling out. The flatcars held carriages and calliopes, big cages on wheels, tents stacked like flat hats.

There was a yelling and dust raising on the tracks as the ponies came down the ramp. Their handlers kept them bunched together as they bristled and clopped.

Poles and tents and other big bundles were carried and loaded on the beds of parked trucks for the drive to the fairground. The animals were being gathered to a spot across the tracks, by the Great Northern warehouse. Yellow weeds grew among the iron rails and the ponies were eating them.

Kristine pointed through the gap in the trains to that spot. "That's where the parade will start. We should get our bicycles and follow them."

"Okay, we'll go. I just want to see an elephant first."

The circus was still pouring from the train in boxes and cages. In one crate a seal was being carefully handed down.

"George!" Kristine squeezed his arm again.

Right next to them, from a window opened in the boxcar a gray elephant trunk wavered out. It hovered, smelled, turned slightly left and right tasting the deep sea-like layers of the air. The coal burned engine ticking upwind had brought Roosevelt to a town that smelled of the ocean and wood pulp, mill and fir trees. And something else…It was close by…The elephant could sense that big summer dream transmitter standing only two feet away. As far as it could reach, the elephant stretched for George.

Ahead of them a band led the way playing some loud marching song, horns and drums, xylophones, followed by jugglers, that man on the stilts, tumblers and dancing girls with flags, the ponies, a camel, elephants, a cage with a lion, clowns and a cart with the seal, more performers, a Saturn Circus banner and at the end was anyone who wanted to join in from the station to the fairground on Iowa and Lincoln Streets.

The circus had touched the ground of town and it made its way down Ohio Street. People came out of their houses and work and stopped their routines to line the sidewalks. They waved and cars stopped at the crossings.

George's bicycle was on a cloud. To be pedaling along a part of the circus, he was right where he felt he belonged. He could even take a hand off the handlebar for a second or two to wobble and wave. Beside him, Kristine was ringing that bell with her thumb, for they were coming up those old cobbled stones past the last edges of neighborhood to the big green field waiting like a tablecloth for the circus to spread out upon.

It would take the rest of the day raising the circus out of the ground. Three great filled canvas tents would be ready for the evening show.

When George and Kristine steered their bicycles

off the city street onto the dirt and grass of the fairground, the circus was already marking off its territory, unloading and unrolling. Everyone was working together to make the Saturn Circus reappear. George noticed even the elephants were pushing the carriages and hauling rolls of canvas and contraptions. It was just like all the books he read; they were one big family. And the circus would pop and bloom for only a night and then move on, blown along by their train from town to town, from one ocean to the other.

George and Kristine parked their bicycles against the soft trunk of a cedar and watched the garden grow. The tall masts of the tents were strung with the ropes driven in the stakes that pulled up the giant sail sides. It's happening! George thought. It's happening right here in our town.

The field had been transformed into a half inflated circus when a shiny red bicycle came around past where the camels were standing.

It was Billy Van Sloat. Dodging bales of hay, he stood on his pedals as he steered towards George and Kristine.

He's showing off, George thought, showing off for the circus.

Billy took his time getting to their cedar tree. He hopped over the frame while the bike was still rolling and landed on the ground. "Hey, George," he said and nodded, "Hello, Kristine."

"Hello," they replied.

Billy held his bike with one hand and shoved his other hand into his pocket, taking out a slip of bright orange paper. "Look what I got. It's a free pass for the show tonight."

"How'd you get that?" George asked.

Billy flashed a grin. "I earned it. I hauled water for the elephants. They were thirsty."

"Lucky…" George said.

Gloating, Billy tucked the pass into his shirt pocket where it stood brightly. "I asked if I could feed the lions, but only the trainer can do that."

"I wouldn't care to feed the lions," Kristine said.

"Yeah, well there's a big sea lion too. I watched them feed it a whole bucket of fish."

"The newspaper said that seal is college educated," George said.

Billy nodded. "He seemed pretty smart alright." Billy swung his leg over his bike. "Anyway, I better get back home now. I'll see you at the show tonight." He tapped his free pass to check that it was still there, then he rode standing tall on his pedals towards where the curb of Lincoln Street began.

"I guess we better get going too," said George. He stood and brushed at the scaly, dried cedar leaves stuck to his jeans. He held Kristine's bicycle out for her to take. Past the field, he watched as Billy Van Sloat hopped his bike off onto the street.

George unleashed his own bicycle from the tree and pushed it over the bumpy ground. There was a bubblegum patch over his front tire. It reappeared slowly as the wheel revolved. Where the fender was broken, you could see it go.

Kristine caught up with him. She sort of laughed for him and added, "I don't see how a seal could go to college though."

In those long summer days of yellow, blue and green light, it stayed warm until the first stars showed. The air seemed thicker then, cooked all day, simmered in leaves, like some thick syrup made of flowers, stirred with spinning bicycle wheels and the sounds of all those children. With the schools closed, those voices were free to play games and their shouts and songs flowed through the neighborhoods like radio waves.

George coasted his rattling bicycle off Ellsworth, over the cut grass, around the Victory Garden. He put his feet down and stopped next to the sailboat overturned below his window and greeted his brother with a, "Hey."

Andrew was sanding the old paint on the hull. The pale wood of the boat showed smooth as a seashell. George crept up closer. He didn't expect much talk from his brother, especially these days with the war weighing him down. Still, George asked him, "What are you doing?"

Andrew's shirt and hands were dusted white as a ghost. He stopped sanding for a moment. "I'm fixing our boat." He had the sandpaper wrapped around a block of wood. Andrew tapped the hull with it. He said, "Filling these seams and resealing it." Then he started sanding again. That sound sort of ended their conversation, but George was used to it. Andrew seemed to be holding back a whole wall of words.

George pushed his bicycle around the corner of the house to the backyard. The tool shed door was still open. The lawnmower was parked inside and there was room for George's bicycle too beside a shelf full of paint and oil cans with a red flying horse. George liked the row of glass jars filled with nails and screws. Further up the wall they were hung to the bottom of a shelf by their lids. It looked like something you'd see in a pet store or an aquarium. They were all different sizes and colored from drab to bright gold. They did seem to swim in their little jars.

George closed the door behind him and padded across the lawn to the kitchen door. White sunlight shined on the glass of it. As soon as that sun started dropping, the circus would begin.

"Hello!" George called out as he turned the door knob and pushed. The kitchen door opened with that familiar click of latch and squeak, a feel and sound he would always recall. He stepped inside the smell of food cooking in the oven and the radio lull from the other room where his parents were talking.

As evening began to fold down, from points all over town, crows made for their roosting trees. Those birds would come one by one, over the roofs and oaks and the roads and alleys and lots. They would find each other in the purple sky and join in with other crows going the same way, so that sometimes you could count a black pebbly stream of them flying overhead fifty at a time, then only a few, then more would fly over again. They flew northeast cawing to each other as they followed their route. They too were looking forward to the fairground with its big poplar trees and maples where they would circle and dive and call out to each other before settling like pepper all over those branches, wings folded in, to rest and sleep.

George and his family were in their car, like so many others, nodding across the bumpy industrial zone roads to the circus fairground. And George was the sort of boy who watched the sky out his backseat window and so he did notice the crows in bunches or handfuls or in ones and twos and threes. They seemed to be showing people where to go. He said quietly, "We're all headed the same place tonight."

The warehouses and railyards were dark for the night, but the fairground made a glow in the distance. It was the same reddish glow you could see at the turn of the century when they used to burn the forests on the edges of town, pushing back that primeval green woods to make room for neighborhoods and planting fields. The circus made that glow with neon signs and rides and roving spotlights. The tents shimmered like paper lanterns.

Cars were parked all along Lincoln and nearest to the fairground every spot along the curb was filled. "Bringing joy and cheer to a troubled world," the newspaper said and there were plenty coming to this big field who needed exactly that. The atmosphere of the fairground was as different a world as another planet. It was true—just across the boundary between city and circus you could feel the change. It was electric.

The crows were surprised by the lights and excitement, the tents and crowds, the animals and rides—such a complete change from yesterday they seemed to lose the power of flight. They dropped and wheeled about like falling black leaves. Before they got their wings working again, some of them fell into the shadows onto the ground. Some of them landed to catch their breath on the taut ropes and pennant flag poles. Most of the crows recovered though and hurried to their roosting trees further across the choppy fairground. The few crows that stayed where they were took in the wonder of this unbelievable night unfolding.

George saw a crow beside a carriage wheel eating fallen popcorn. He watched it hop and fly as they passed on the way to the big top. The crowds also eddied off to slow past the stands selling food and toys and souvenirs. There stood a wooden theater with the carved likenesses of Hollywood stars. A magician held a flower that blew up in his hand. A strongman braced himself, wrapped tight in chains like the paper ones on a Christmas tree.

A crow almost landed on the roof of a calliope until the pipes burst into a hooting popular Glenn Miller song.

A woman carrying a big camera with a flash called out, "Get your picture taken with Roosevelt the elephant! Souvenir of the circus! Fifteen cents!"

A man pushed a cart packed with goldfish bowls. There were cheers from the tents at the ponies trotting round, at the clowns and acrobats, the crack of a whip and a lion's roar. There was the elephant show and the seal with his horns and way up high on the wire strung between poles the trapeze family took a bow.

When George had seen every tent show, he stopped to watch W.C Fields and Mae West puppets, got a photo taken beside an elephant and was so full of circus it overflowed, then he followed his family back towards the car. Yes, he loved the circus, but it was almost too much to record. Every corner, everywhere, every sense was boiling, a million times over. And maybe for the first time he wondered how it would be for an animal.

George held that photograph of the elephant and him safe under his coat, walking like Napoleon. Lincoln Street was that curtain parted where they left the noise of the bands and calliope and all that fevered neon and returned to town.

It seemed over all too quick to George. They were on a dark street without light, just what fell from the moon and stars. They walked past a construction yard surrounded by an iron fence. Piles of lumber were stacked in the gloom, the perfect setting for a mystery. Maybe that oily looking puddle was really a watery tunnel leading out to the sea where a submarine awaited a shipment of two-by-four pines. George saw another crow float dimly off the zinc roof. Part of him hoped it was actually a bat following a radio signal to a gang of spies…the sort of plot that happened in shadows on the screen at double feature matinees.

George's father found the car and opened the door for his wife. Andrew got in one side in back and George in the other door. His father took off his hat, tossed it on the dashboard and got behind the wheel. "Well, George," he said. "Was that enough circus for a year?"

George said something in a yawn. His voice from the back seat came from much further away. He was covered in tent, riding on rails, washing an elephant big as a house.

The car turned onto Iowa Street. It crossed James. The windows were rolled down just enough to let in that cool watery pour of summer evening.

The radio went on, and George's father tuned the dial.

"The axis steam roller continues to crush through Southern Russia, approaching the Volga at a ferocious speed of fire and bloodshed. Military observers maintain there is little doubt a decisive encounter awaits beyond the Don river bend at the city of Stalingrad."

Looking out the window, George thought of those cities in Europe and Asia that were on fire. On this very night, bombs were falling on them. He wondered what they would do if it happened here? Pull the car over, run holding hands, run and run and run…

His mother reached forward and turned the radio

41

off.

The tires bumped over railroad tracks and the black cobblestones flecked by the light of the orange moon.

George wanted to stay awake. He wanted to hold onto all those circus feelings while they were still so strong. He knew that sleep would start to wash them away. The edges would be worn like a sandcastle until eventually he might only remember a night in July when he was ten and he saw the circus...A sentence for what had been a two hour long dream happening.

With the bedside lamp on, George stared at the photograph propped under the light. He was standing there beside Roosevelt. He remembered the feel of the elephant skin, like a tree or clay that had grown from the ground.

He wondered what Roosevelt was doing now and how they got all those animals to settle down to sleep. Maybe it was easy...Maybe all that elephant needed was the lamps turned off? Roosevelt would close those big eyes and see visions start to form. Those things we call dreams would free him from that chain that staked him to the ground...Roosevelt would move like a cloud, lift the tent flap and that big shadow would drift along, unseen past the caravan where the clowns played cards...past the lion cage, the dark puppet show caravan. Roosevelt was going out into the night and George would meet him...

Yawning, George lifted his arm with his last remaining strength to pull the string to turn off his bedside light.

The next morning, there was no bird whistle or Morse code rap on his windowsill to awaken George. Uncle Robert didn't pay him an early dawn visit, so George slept until the sunshine woke him.

When he opened his eyes, the first thing he saw was the photograph of Roosevelt and him. He thought of the circus and the second thing he thought was, "They're leaving today!"

George shot out of bed. He stumbled out of the blanket. He dragged and hopped from that cloth to the dresser drawers. As fast as he could he put on clothes, but he couldn't get rid of the thought that he would be too late, that he would get to the fairground and find only some sawdust circles and the holes in the ground that held the tent city down.

It only took him a minute to get dressed—he hoped that wasn't too long.

"George! For heaven's sake, what's got into you?" his mother cried as she stepped aside in the hall.

He ran past her, saying, "I have to get to the fairground! The circus is leaving!"

Those eleven words carried him rocket-speed from the hallway and out the front door. Down the steps, across the lawn, he jumped the morning *Herald* resting next to the only dandelion to survive yesterday's mowing.

"You've got to eat something!" his mother called.

George ran around the corner of the house and slid into the tool shed, opening the door with a flick of his hand.

Even in such a hurry, he took a moment to plant his feet in that stillness in there—the smell of the lawnmower and engine oil and the sleepy sunlight that lived in there. He grabbed his bicycle and guided it out, turning the handlebars this way then that, and backing it out onto the grass.

Like the Lone Ranger, George threw himself onto the seat, dug his feet into the pedals, circling, finding speed, churning past the garden, bumping over the sidewalk on his way to where he hoped the circus would still be.

Every time someone in a movie needs to get somewhere quick, you see a silver airplane dashing across the globe. That's how George pictured his morning travel. His bicycle had sprouted wings, with big radial motors spinning propellers, humming him over city streets.

On Iowa he saw the poplar trees that marked the edge of the fairground, but none of those tents broke through the horizon of green meadow. It suddenly dawned on him that he was too late. The circus had folded up and blown town. Only the smell of it lingered on.

George glided up Lincoln, along the curb, the airplane vanishing, replaced by a bicycle with leg pistons, burning tired from that frantic ride. He panted and slowed by the trampled earth, stopped by a hole big enough to be an elephant footprint.

Gazing across the fairground, he caught his breath. Lit by the morning, it resembled the quiet of a dead battleground. How could the circus disappear without him there to say goodbye?

The field had been cleared of all that was there last night except for one funny looking structure. It was like a sentry box, or a shoebox tent stood on end. George let his squeaking bicycle glide him toward it.

When he was closer he could read black letters, SATURN CIRCUS, painted on its canvas.

The fairgrounds were so quiet though, just the sound of his bicycle. A couple crows on the far side of the field flew towards town.

George planted his feet and stopped his bike beside the tent. It had an entry, a flap that was tied closed with some strings. George wondered if he should look inside. "Hello?" he called.

What would he see if he looked in there? The tent was no bigger than a phone booth. In fact, he thought that's what the circus canvas could be covering…a disguised telephone booth. What if he heard a telephone start to ring? If he unstitched those knots and went in, who would he be talking to on the other end of the line? Did the magician he saw last night really know more than card tricks and sleight of hand? Had he miniaturized the entire circus and sent them zinging by telephone wire to the next city south, marched them out of some other phone booth there, in another vacant lot?

George tried, "Hello?" one last time. Brave as he liked to imagine he could be, he couldn't bring himself to look inside that wardrobe-sized tent.

He started to pedal again, his thick balloon tires biting into the sawdust, spent cigarettes and bottle caps as a cry drifted towards him on the air.

George turned to see the bluff of tall trees where the crows slept nights, and he spotted a lone figure approaching. In the haze of the summer field it looked like a flower was walking his way.

No wonder George thought it was a flower growing closer…Mel Tell wore oversized, bright green trousers held up by red suspenders, a lemon yellow shirt with blue buttons and a huge white cowboy hat. He looked like he had been painted into the field or colored into life with crayons. When he stopped to mop his brow with the polka-dot handkerchief he pulled from his sleeve, George recognized him as one of the three clowns starring in Saturn Circus. The Friday *Herald* even had a photo of him that had been pasted into George's notebook.

Mel saluted the boy and sat down with a sigh on the chair beside his tent. He pointed a thumb behind him. "Kid, I been all up and down this park…No sign of him…" The clown peeled off his shoes and dropped them like canoes on the grass.

"Who are you looking for?"

"Roosevelt…One of our elephants…" He wiped his brow again and stuffed the handkerchief back up his sleeve. "He got off his chain sometime last night."

George whistled, "Jeepers…" It was a word Kristine liked to use.

"Yeah," the clown agreed. "When Roosevelt got loose in Santa Rosa he was gone for two days. We found him in a cornfield."

"He gets loose a lot?"

"Whenever he can. He acts like he doesn't want to be in the circus anymore."

"Really?"

Mel shrugged.

George stared at the field, thinking. "What happened to the rest of the circus?"

"They left me to find Roosevelt. The show must go on, kid. Once I find him, they'll send a truck to pick us up."

"What if you don't find him?"

The clown made a knife motion across his throat, tongue hanging out. Then he laughed, "No, he's out there somewhere. An elephant can't just vanish. I've been looking for hours though...I need a break." Mel stood up. "Say, are you hungry, kid?"

George nodded. "I didn't have any breakfast. I rushed out here to see the circus."

"Yep. That's what I figured. You wait right here." The clown untied the flap of the tent. George could see a jumble of things stashed in there. It looked like Mel was prepared for a couple days hunt.

First, Mel brought out another folding chair for the boy, then a collapsible table which he opened and settled between the chairs. He returned to the tent once more and came back with a black suitcase which he laid on the table. "The magician loaned me this..." he said with a wink.

When Mel flicked the latches and opened the lid,

George gave a surprised gasp. There were two plates with toast and jam and a steaming silver coffee pot.

"Jeepers, right?" Mel said.

George nodded slowly.

Mel passed him a plate and poured him a half cup of coffee. "Not sure if you like coffee. If you do, you probably like it with plenty of sugar and cream, I bet." He dropped in two sugar cubes and from a pocket of the suitcase removed a small pitcher of milk. He gave the cup a stir and passed it to George.

"Thanks." George set the cup on the table. He didn't want to admit he never had coffee before. He picked up a piece of toast instead. It was covered with strawberry jam and tasted as good as he hoped it would. George also didn't want to ask how the breakfast suitcase worked—he knew magicians never gave away their secrets.

Mel sat down across from George with his coffee and toast. "Wouldn't you think an elephant would leave a trail a mile wide? Not Roosevelt…" Mel took a sip from his cup. "Of course, moving the circus out of here took care of any tracks." He tried a bite of his toast. He didn't seem to be in a hurry at all. "But sooner or later, somebody will see him. He'll show up in somebody's back yard, or a school playground."

George took a sip of his own coffee. It tasted like tree bark. No amount of sugar and cream could disguise it.

George must have made a face because Mel

laughed. He reached into the suitcase again and found a glass of orange juice. "Here…Try this."

"Thanks." There would be time for coffee years from now, and George would think of Mel Tell every time he had a cup. On this summer morning in 1942 though, the orange juice was so good George finished the glass in three quick sips. He was done with his toast too.

Mel put their dishes and cups back in the suitcase and shut the lid.

George expected to hear a clatter as Mel lifted it and carried the bag back to the tent, but the silence reminded him it was not any ordinary suitcase.

Mel set the suitcase down just inside the tent and took something off a shadow. He came back to the table and held the object out on his hand for George. "Here, you can have this."

"What is it?"

"It's an elephant caller."

George turned the small wooden horn around to look at it.

"You blow through it. Roosevelt will hear it and come to you."

George tried it and only the wind of his breath came through. "I didn't hear anything," he told Mel.

"An elephant hears tones we can't hear," Mel explained. "That horn carries a hundred yards or so, maybe more on a good breeze."

George pointed it at the horizon and tried again.

He saw the black speck of a crow leave the fairground trees for town. Maybe Mel didn't know where to look for an elephant, but a crow would know where Roosevelt went. Crows kept track of everything going on in town.

George pocketed the elephant caller in his coat pocket and said, "Thanks, Mr. Tell. I'll see if I can find Roosevelt." He got back on his bicycle.

"See you around, kid."

George bumped over the ground. It had been swept by the outgoing circus but he remembered the clue he saw when he rode in. Amid all the scrabble and trample there was an elephant footprint walking out.

George stopped his bicycle on the corner of James Street and tested the elephant caller. Then he listened…for a rustle in the overgrown weeds, the crinkling of the chain link fence, for footsteps big enough to rattle the pebbles on the road. But there was nothing to hear but the morning. Still, now that he looked at the city as a place for an elephant to hide, it seemed there was plenty of possibility. An empty garage with the door left open would be wide enough to store Roosevelt for a while.

George returned the caller to his pocket, gave his bike a push and started to pedal. He would have done this for hours, inching about the map of town, stopping every once in a while to call Roosevelt's name, until he heard his own name yelled from an alley.

"George!"

George turned his handlebars that way and saw Billy Van Sloat.

"George!"

"What?"

Billy coasted standing on his pedals out of the alley. He braked his shiny bicycle hard so his thick back tire gave a shriek. Everyone knew you weren't supposed to waste rubber.

"I have an important mission for us," Billy said.

George kept quiet. He didn't want to say he was already on one—he really didn't want Billy knowing about Roosevelt.

"Follow me," Billy told him.

George hesitated. There were still blocks to cover looking for Roosevelt. He had barely begun.

Billy turned around. "We have to hurry up. I don't know how long it's going to stay there. Come on!"

This time as he pedaled, George was pulled along. It was like the alley was filled with rushing water and George couldn't fight the current. There were ferns growing in the cool spaces between parked cars and garages—he couldn't have grabbed hold—they would only have raked through his fingers as he flew by helplessly.

They caught the trolley on Kentucky Street going east. Billy got the seat by the window. George sat next to him on the aisle.

This wasn't the first time they rode the rails. Last spring, Billy and his brother got George to hop an open freight car with them and it took them an hour east before they could jump off and call home. At least this was only a trolley, on a fixed route, going out to the lake and back.

Once Billy was assured the driver was not George's father, he relaxed and withdrew a crumpled *Herald* article from his shirt pocket. "Did you see this?" He passed it to George, keeping it low, below the level of the seat in case the old lady ahead of them took notice.

George was sure he hadn't seen the article. All he read in the paper were the circus notices and the daily comics. Still, Billy's article looked interesting and he read it slowly and peaceably as Billy let him alone and the wheels clicked on the tracks and the trolley creaked and belled along.

Model Airplane Contest. For Boys and Girls of This County. Details of a model airplane contest being sponsored by the Civilian Defense organization held to provide models of American and Axis warplanes for use in training ground observers of the warcraft warning service. "In *order to have a properly trained personnel on plane watch here," a spokesman said, "It is necessary for watchers to be able to distinguish immediately between enemy and friendly planes flying over observed areas. Many model plane-builders have skill that will make them an important part of the air defense of this region. Here is a chance for boys and girls who have been building model planes for fun to take a definite part in our war effort and at the same time to compete for worthwhile prizes offered." Rules and entry blanks may be obtained in the court house, the Chamber of Commerce, the Standard Auto Company, and from defense council members in the county. Prizes will include a first prize of $15; second prize, $10; third, fourth and fifth prizes, $5 each, and sixth and seventh prizes, $2.50 each.*

As George finished reading, he let the scrap of paper curl on his hand like a dead leaf.

Billy leaned over to say in a loud whisper, "My brother and I are going to win that first prize." He put the crumpled article back in his shirt and patted the pocket flat. "You just wait and see."

The trolley passed into a stand of tall fir trees. It got dark as the sunlight was blocked out and the light inside turned green as an aquarium.

"How much further are we going," said George.

"To the lake. You're not going to believe what I found there." He got quieter again, in case that old lady was really a spy. "You can't tell anyone about this though."

"Okay, okay." George looked out the window across the aisle. When the trees made a forest like that, he thought of the Indian paths that must run quietly through. Out the windshield were specks of blue light in the branches. The trolley began to descend and bank like an airplane nearing the airport.

The boys walked on the gravel edge of the road. Tall yellow and green weeds, foxglove and blackberry thickets grew down to the shore. There was little traffic on the road. A sedan went by earlier and the driver held out his arm to wave.

"I see the path," Billy said at last.

George wanted to say something out loud about all the elephant time this journey was costing but he kept quiet, following Billy off the pebbly slope onto the dirt path into the woods.

Small birds were hiding and singing around in the alder canopy. A squirrel bounded away from them and launched itself at a tree. Billy was too slow with the stone he picked up to throw. George knew the squirrel would hide on the other side of the tree until they were gone. Billy threw his rock anyway, out into the thick growing tangle where it snapped in the underbrush.

George thought the path would take them right down to the lake where whatever it was would be. Instead, another five minutes of walking went by as they followed the shoreline, kept hidden in all the leaves.

This reminded George of another adventure with Billy Van Sloat. At the gravel pit, he and Billy had found a buried car tire in the mud. It was something they could have brought to the rubber drive. They imagined there might have been more under there too…at least three, for the rest of the car. And what if it was only the tip of a whole underground tower of them? They tried for an hour to get it out but never got it more than halfway. Their hands were left scratched and raw.

Billy spotted some poison ivy to their right and made a big deal about not touching it, as if the low plant was crouched, ready to spring. He found a snapped branch and used it to poke the ivy. "Hah!" he cried out as he lanced at the shiny plant.

George told him, "Leaves of three, let it be."

Billy held the branch in the air as if its broken tip dripped with deadly poison. He waved it close to George, laughed, then tossed it to the trees.

"C'mon," Billy said. "We're almost there." He surveyed the forest leaning against their path. "Now we have to be quiet." He sort of crouched as he led George, the way the soldiers did in the movies.

The path had narrowed to the width of their shoes and the prickly salal grabbed at them. Billy started to fall but caught the rough bark of a tree with a slap of his hand. The path turned into a scramble of dirt and rocks tumbling ten steep feet to the shore.

They landed loudly on a beach of smooth round shiny stones. The path kept coming after them in a trickle of loosened earth and dust.

Billy held a finger up to hush George. They stood

there frozen, listening to the rhythmic lap of the water. It almost sounded like a code.

Shifting his feet in the stones, Billy motioned for George to follow him, slowly. Their shoes sunk a little into each step, not exactly silently, as they crept towards a great fallen cedar tree. It had been chopped out from the forest into the lake like a dock. Like a wall, it was tall enough that it hid the beach on the other side.

Billy touched his lips again and with a craning turn of his hand showed George they would have to go over the tree. He took a few crunching steps along the trunk to where the soft reddish bark could be climbed.

George used the same clefts and stood beside Billy at the top. They had to walk down the slanting trunk where it dived into the water. Stopped before that reflection of rippling blue sky, Billy turned to look at the beach. George stopped too, planting his shoes as best he could.

"It's gone!"

"What?" George only saw more of the shore and crowds of trees.

"The seaplane! There was a Japanese Yokosuka seaplane right there on the beach!" Billy pushed around George, nearly knocking him into the lake, to get to where he could drop off the cedar onto the shore.

George watched him run across the damp stones and stop.

"It was right here!" He held out his arms like

wings. "They had it camouflaged with branches and stuff." He looked around him on the beach and picked up a bough from a fir. "See! Here's one!" Billy kicked at the stones. "Here's the tracks from the floats…It was resting right here."

Billy ran his shoe along a furrow and stopped where the lake began, at a thin line of foam and bits of bark. "They must have got scared…Maybe they knew I saw their plane."

"Yeah," said George. "Maybe."

"Sure," Billy agreed, but his voice trailed off as he looked to the sky. "What's that noise?"

George thought he was looking for another Japanese plane. There were a few dots of crows on the far side of the lake. The sunlight shined on a house window like a diamond in the trees. Then George felt the rumble too.

It got louder. Airplanes, stacked together in bird-like formation came low over the lake from the south. They were huge, four engines roaring, humming the water's surface, filling the space that was blue and cloud.

"B-17s!" Billy yelled. He lay flat on the ground, digging his hands in the stones.

George clung to the cedar. The sound of the bombers was so loud it sawed.

More of them came, flat dark wings burred over-head. They were so low George could see the windows, the turrets and guns, the painted stars and the bomb bay doors were open. He screamed to make it stop. He pressed his face against the cedar's soft bark.

The whole bowl of the lake was filled with the boiling engine thrum of the B-17s. George begged it to stop, held to the tree and waited to be dead.

But the planes passed onward overhead and the sound of them turned like thunder back into the clouds, the wind, the water brushing onto a beach and the hiss of half a billion leaves.

"With his faithful valet Kato, Britt Reid, daring young publisher, matches wits with racketeers and saboteurs, risking his life that criminals and enemy spies will feel the weight of the law by the sting of the Green Hornet! Ride with Britt Reid in a thrilling adventure, The Invisible Enemy! The Green Hornet Strikes again!" The buzzing car turned into a fanfare and George got up off the floor. That was his space by the radio. With eyes closed, he would listen completely, practically fall in to the other world created by sound.

He went to the kitchen and stood there, caught in the last sunlight of the day. Already down around the trunks of the trees it was turning dark. In the summer his parents would let him go free. Summer was his vacation, and he could fly like a kite, day or night.

"George?" his mother called him from the other room. "Are you alright?"

"I'm okay," he said.

He wasn't done with the day. There were always so many things you wish you did, especially in these summer days which were like gold.

He put his hand on the silver faucet and poured some water in a glass that was waiting by the sink. He filled it up and watched as the current became invisible again.

From the living room came the show on the radio and the murmur of his parents along with it. Against the cooled touch of the window glass above the faucet he could almost feel the songs of those last birds of the day singing the same way they did in the morning, completing the circle, making the glass their very own kind of metal, created in air and suspended on their kitchen wall.

"I'll be right back," George called to the other room. "I forgot my baseball glove at the park." He opened the door, that memory door, and slipped out quickly into the dusk.

He was on his bicycle again, pedaling, coasting. The broad leaves of the maples over the sidewalk, like holding hands, were painted by the setting sun. George turned on Girard Street. It wasn't exactly the place he was going but he hadn't seen Kristine all day. He just wanted to see her, that's all…Especially after a day like today. There was something about being near her that was okay.

He saw her house and he bumped right over the lawn around the flowering apple tree. There were lights on. Her bicycle was parked beside the red steps on the front porch. That's where he stopped and leaned his bike next to hers.

He stopped and listened. Now that he wasn't riding his creaking, clattery bicycle, he could hear the neighborhood. Besides the birds, there were all the radios on, a slight and fading blend of music, laughter and voices linked together like a paperclip chain tied from house to house on into the distance.

George didn't go up the stairs to her door, he went around the side of her house, past the rhododendron and daisies. He was pretty sure she would be on the porch in the backyard. Sure enough, she was.

She was standing at her easel, painting.

"Hi, Kristine."

"George! You surprised me." There was white paint on her hand.

"Sorry." He paused at the wooden stairs. "What are you doing?"

"Painting, silly." She stepped back from the easel and pointed with the brush. "I painted a circus elephant. Now I'm making stars on it. The last star is a little jumpy, thanks to you."

"Oops."

"Would you like some lemonade? We've got a pitcher of it."

"Okay," George said then wandered up the steps and opened the screen door and stood beside the rocking chair next to a table set with glasses, spoons and a yellow half full pitcher.

"Help yourself," Kristine called. She started another white star on the elephant.

George took a glass from the black lacquered serving tray and picked up the heavy pitcher with both hands and poured. The sound made him instantly thirsty. Before he tried it, he turned to see her painting.

Of course he liked anything to do with elephants. Still, he couldn't believe how much he loved her painting. He wished he would have painted it, put those colors together like that, flowed the shape of that big elephant in among all those trees and flowers and topped it all off with stars. Even that star he had jumped her into painting was perfect.

Then he took a sip of the lemonade. It was so sour his mouth hung open like a goldfish.

She noticed his face and laughed. "I forgot to tell you, the lemonade doesn't have any sugar."

The sugar ration, he remembered. His mother had been talking about it too. Soon there might not be anything sweet. George managed to forget how lemonade used to taste and he swallowed with effort and said, "It's still good."

"If you say so." She took a step back from the easel and tilted her red hair to look at the painting the way artists are supposed to do.

"Do you want to go to the fairground with me?"

"Now?"

"I was there this morning. There's still a clown there. He's looking for a lost elephant."

"Really?" she said. "I heard about that."

George was going to show her the elephant caller. It was still in his coat pocket. He didn't get the chance. The door to the house opened and George jumped the way Kristine had a minute ago.

"George," Kristine's mother said. She turned on a porch light. "What a nice surprise."

"I just came by to see Kristine," he said. "I should go though." He set the glass on the tray. "Thanks for the lemonade."

"You're welcome any time, George," said Kristine's mother.

"Bye, George."

He had his feet on the steps as he answered, "I'll see you tomorrow, Kristine." He hopped over the last step and landed on the grass. The sky was turning plum. The backyard was pooling with shadow. The lights on her porch shone like the bridge of a steamship plowing into night. Kristine stood on the deck at the wheel, her easel. "I like your painting."

He heard her say, "Thanks," as he was leaving along the side of her house.

In a moment he was on his bicycle again.

The fairground was a blue lake hiding in the color of the night sky. Mel's tent glowed like a lantern. As George neared, he could see the clown sitting on that same camp chair outside. It looked like he hadn't moved since George left. Maybe he didn't need to though. George wondered if the clown had a crystal ball, another loan from the magician, and maybe all he needed to do was look into that eye to rove and search every elephant hiding place around town.

George called out, "Hello!" as he arrived, though he was sure Mel heard the bicycle and saw his silhouette against the lights of town.

Mel raised his arm and waved slowly, a red glow from a cigar he held made a scratch in the night.

"Welcome back to the Saturn Circus outpost," Mel said.

George parked his bicycle in the same spot. "No elephant yet?"

"Roosevelt remains on the loose. Have a seat." He poked a long shoe at George's old chair. "Right after you left this morning, some newspaper men showed up. A radio fellow too. Roosevelt is probably the talk of the town by now."

"I wouldn't know. I was out looking all day."

"No luck with the elephant caller?"

"There's still a lot of places to try."

"That's right. I got a lead. Roosevelt might have been seen up there on the Indian reservation. There's a bunch of woods around there. Say, are you hungry? I think there's still some stew left in the suitcase."

"No. No thank you. I should get back home now anyway. I just wanted to see if Roosevelt got found."

Mel stood up with him. "I'll let you know. What's your name, kid?"

"George." He shook Mel's glove. "I'll come by tomorrow if that's okay."

"Of course. Anytime."

George got on his bicycle. It was growing harder to see those holes and ruts on the fairground.

"Goodnight, George."

"Goodnight."

By the time he got home it was very night. Putting his bike away in the shed, George knocked a hammer down from somewhere. He tripped a little on the way to the steps lit by the kitchen door window. He turned the handle like some jewel thief testing a bank vault, dialing it just until it clicked and giving it a gentle pull.

George paused in the kitchen. The radio was still on in the other room. "Well, that's act one of the tonight's *Thin Man* case. And now, during intermission, let's hear from tonight's special guest, Tommy Dorsey and his Orchestra. We're certainly glad you accepted our invitation, Tommy and we're turning the spotlight on you while you play one of those swell arrangements that have made you famous. The stage is yours, Tommy." After a fanfare, George recognized the song, "I Can't Give You Anything But Love."

He decided he couldn't have been gone too long. Usually he was on his way to bed by this time or begging to stay up a little more, but this was summer and why should it matter when the nights were warm and school didn't exist in the morning.

"George?" his mother called.

"I'm home."

"We were beginning to wonder." His mother met

him as he walked in to the parlor where his father sat with the big radio playing music. It seemed the only time George ever saw his father was at night, when he came home from a long day at work.

"You didn't run into that elephant out there?" his father asked.

"I wish," George said, "Some people think it might be on the reservation."

"Uncle Robert said one of the trains spotted it this afternoon." His mother squeezed George's shoulder as she gave him a kiss on his soft hair. She began to guide him down the hall towards his room. "Uncle Robert asked if you'd like to see a movie with him tomorrow? He said there's a circus in it."

"Oh, yeah?…Maybe."

"I told him it sounded too scary for you." She kissed the top of his head again. "He said you'd like it. Of course, he's already seen it ten times or so."

"Why does Uncle Robert get to watch movies all day? And go the train station and do whatever he wants to?"

"Honestly, George," she sighed. "Sometimes you sound just like your father."

"I heard that!" came a voice from the other room, like it was spun on shellac and played from the radio.

George laughed. "Goodnight, Dad!"

The clock spun the room underwater deeper in the deep blue color of night. The clock on the bookshelf ticked, its hands a slow propeller turning time, pushing George through another dream. He was on his bicycle. It was right where he was earlier, riding home from the fairground, pedaling hard against the thick syrup of nighttime, when he pulled on the handlebars and soared off the ground. Below him the fairground was a field of stars, every dandelion in the grass shining a web of lights.

George leveled off at the height of the telephone poles. With ease, he could ride on the wires like a cable car. He followed a wire right to the peak of a gabled house and he rolled off onto the shingled roof. Up there on that island the backs of all the houses rose out of the black. Downtown were the movie theaters, the tall Leopold Hotel with its radio tower and red light blinking on top.

George got his elephant caller from his pocket and blew. His breath going through came out as an elephant trumpet. It sent a wave of bright sound rippling out and George listened for a reply. His bicycle didn't wait for one. It grew wings, black as a crow's and suddenly George was flying again, turned by the wind in a wide circle over the sleeping town.

He blew the caller. He searched the streets and rails, the map beneath his flapping broad wings. Then he heard the sound echoed back. His bicycle-bird veered towards the reply, over a row of creaking, slow moving railway cars. George stuck a foot out to kick past a streetlamp, as he veered over the Cornwall bridge.

The concrete stopped where the city dropped off into a cool, dark ravine of trees. This was where the creek ran through town, winding from the lake, back and forth between neighborhoods to empty in the bay.

George settled in the crown of an oak, the wings tucked and folded, and he could see the ribbon of water gliding through the branches. It was a beautiful spot, like a place in a Tarzan movie. The elephant, painted purple and blue and dotted with white stars, looked up at George for only a moment—conveying the urgency, the fear, the need to escape and hide away—then reached for a shadow. Like turning a page, the elephant pulled the shadow over itself and the whole night went black. George was wrapped up in a crow. The dream was over.

The clock in his room ticked. He turned in his sleep. A circus book fell off his bed and clacked on the floor. It made a tent shape. Some words had spilled from it, jittering about like ants. The tiny music from the covers drifted out, calliopes and a brass band riding on the roof of a horse drawn carriage. George followed the script and sound right into another dream, one he knew by heart, where he was the boy who ran away with the circus. The only change in the dream was the empty space in the tent where the elephant had been.

Roosevelt had been busy. The radio was buzzing with the news. Even the Seattle stations, strong signals tuned in from miles away, after reporting the war on the Eastern Front and the ships being sunk in the Pacific, couldn't resist the story happening up north where an elephant escaped the circus. Roosevelt was gone but not unseen. Reports came in through the night.

Three Victory Gardens and a chicken coop in the York neighborhood had been raided and uprooted. A rainbarrel was emptied on Potter Street. Washlines in Eldridge had been plowed through by something powerful enough to also push down wooden fences. Huge, round footprints marched across Bayview Cemetery. Two sailors on shore leave swore they saw Roosevelt crossing the street in the fog. Perhaps the most spectacular story of all concerned Maurice Spry, who woke up in the middle of the night to see a gigantic shape with an eye looking in his bedroom window. It huffed and puffed like a fairy tale wolf and shook the glass with its breath. Scrambling outside in his pajamas, Maurice grabbed the axe off his porch to do battle with the demon. When he saw it was an elephant, with no intention of leaving his apple tree feast, Maurice threw the entire woodpile at the beast before it stomped away.

George listened wide-eyed and as the announcer returned the radio to music, he quickly finished his cereal.

His mother had left a white bowl of cut strawberries on the tablecloth. He eyed them, but didn't dare finish them. They were worth more than gold. From a vault in the icebox, they were the last strawberries from the Yamato farm. The war had shut their farm down and taken the Yamatos away. Three red strawberries remained in a snowy bowl.

George pushed his chair back from the table and took his coat off the hook by the door. When he put it on, he checked to make sure the elephant caller was still in the pocket. After all those radio reports, he felt sure half the town would be rigging traps and lures and lines all over, fishing for that elephant. He had an advantage though. He felt the shape of the caller and smiled. He could communicate with Roosevelt. Also, he remembered the dream he had.

The door chirped and squeaked and opened and let him go hop out over the steps to the soft backyard. He stood there warm, watching the snails race for the garden.

His mother was out there in a beam of sunshine, putting clothes on the line. "George," she said, "I suppose you and every other boy and girl in the county will be out gallivanting after that elephant, but don't forget—Uncle Robert would like to meet you at the Grand Theatre at one o'clock."

"Okay."

"Here, before you go, help me with this." She pulled a wet sheet out of the basket set on the grass.

George grabbed one side of it and held it up as high as he could as she lifted the rest of the sail to pin it to the line.

"Thank you, dear."

George wiped his damp hands across his jeans. "Mom. Do you think they would shoot Roosevelt?"

"Heavens no! The circus wants him back safe and sound. He's part of their family." She made the sheet taught so the hours of breeze would press and warm it with sunlight and make it dry by afternoon.

A block from his house, George stopped on the corner and blew the elephant caller. Of course it only sounded like his breath to him, but he could imagine those great elephant ears picking it up and turning that beast his way.

From down the street a black dog suddenly appeared on the sidewalk, so quickly that it looked thrown there. It froze, staring at George from a distance, with one front leg crooked in the air. In slow motion the dog put his foot down and started towards George.

He knew the dogs in his neighborhood he rode through, which were nice, which yards had ones that would rush the fence, which ones were all bark or would put up a chase. This dog, with its head bent low, stalking him, coming closer, George had never seen before. The sight of it creeping almost like a wolf tracking him made George quickly pocket the caller and stand on his pedal to get his bike moving fast.

He hopped the curb and picked up speed on Grand Avenue. In the street he ran his bicycle along the parked cars. He was afraid to look behind, the last thing he wanted to see was that ferocious dog snapping a bite at his tire or heel.

George came to the café at nearly full speed

and turned his front wheel into the alley. Sliding on the dirt, the handlebars jerked twice as he somehow steadied and steered out of a crash, riding up onto the grassy edge siding of the building. He stopped and threw an arm against the warm wall. The dust and his ragged nerves calmed. He was glad there were no windows on this alley side of the café. He thought he must have looked like a complete maniac.

George stepped shakily off his bicycle. He had to lean on the yellow wall.

As he caught his breath and time managed to tighten down out of its unsprung panic, George listened. It sounded like that mad energy that had bounced him up to the café had gone on spinning like a gyroscope and turned into an argument inside the café.

Another ten feet or so from George was a screen door. He bent from the wall to see the sign nailed to the wooden slat: We Don't Serve Elephants. There were two men in there. One of them had just stopped shouting. The other one started to talk in a calmer voice.

George edged along the wall towards the door to hear. It still wasn't easy to walk—his rubber band legs, dragging his feet.

Now he could see the corner of a milk truck parked in the lot just behind the café. Its big gleaming headlight watched George like an eye.

"No!" the man with the shouting voice interrupted the other man's radio-like voice.

Only five feet away, George threw both arms flat against the hot wall as the screen door banged open like the crack of a gunshot.

George saw the milkman, the same milkman who delivered the milk and cream to their house, Bill Wright, stepping backwards out the door. He held up his empty bottle basket between himself and the furious cook.

The cook in his white apron and flailing hands and red face looked about a second away from throwing his fists at Bill.

George, trying to be nothing more than paint on the wall, held his breath.

Bill said in that calm smooth voice of his, "This war didn't just happen. It's never stopped. And until human life is deemed more valuable than money in the bank, until those who seek to profit from war are finally stopped in their tracks, there will never be an end to this war."

"Get out!" the cook bellowed. "Get out of my café and never come back!" He reached for something inside the kitchen.

George took a quick gasp of air. His fingers were rooted in the wooden siding.

"Take your damn papers with you!" The cook threw a bound stack of newsprint at Bill who caught the block in his chest and staggered. "And take your milk!"

There was a terrible clinking and scrape of glass milk bottles as the cook scooped the day's delivery off his counter inside and heaved them out the screen door.

They exploded into white pools and shards in the alley.

"That's for all our boys overseas!" the cook roared at Bill, "They're not talking, they're fighting! And they're dying for this country!"

Bill eased back from the cook. His sky blue uniform was splattered with milk. He held the bundle of his newspapers and the wire birdcage-like carrier.

George could read the look on Bill's face—there were so many words waiting that he could have said, but he held them—George thought of that photograph of Abraham Lincoln on the classroom wall. Bill had that kind of face. And George watched invisibly as Bill turned his back on the cook and in a steady, fearless stride returned to the milk truck parked behind the café.

George stuck to the wall and waited for it all to be over.

The cook slammed the screen door shut going back into his kitchen.

Bill started his truck. The engine whined into reverse and the wheels popped on the gravel as he spun the truck around. Then, with a clunk, he dropped it into forward gear. The milk truck went right by George in a blur.

George stayed painted to the wall. He stared at the ground where the milk bottles exploded, frozen, until all the white had sunk into the dirt and left only dark mottled scars and glass.

George could hear the pots and pans in the kitchen, water running, loud dance music. The screen door was like a radio speaker, with the cook inside some gangster character out of Bulldog Drummond.

As George tried to move again, he realized his heart hadn't stopped racing since his bike almost crashed. Stuffed with frayed wires and loose electricity, George let go of the café and took his first steps away. He could only hope that the cook wasn't coming back with one more milk bottle to throw while George staggered to his bicycle, waiting for him like a trusty mare in a Western show.

As he put his leg over and sat on the seat and pushed against the force of gravity, George forgot all about seeing that black dog that had driven him here.

George knew where the elephant was. The dream had told him. He didn't need to ride in circles. It was just…he didn't know what to do. He sat on his bicycle, hands on the guardrail of State Street as he stared at the deep green ravine where the creek ran through the middle of town.

Maybe it was something the elephant told him last night. Roosevelt didn't want to go back, he didn't want to be found, he wanted to be free.

But how could he? George thought. Roosevelt couldn't go on raiding and taking whatever he liked. He would make enemies. They would come after him—they already were—and when they caught him there might be a fate worse than the circus. A trouble making elephant could expect to be killed.

George pedaled to the next place to stop, an umbrella shaped cherry tree on the corner of Ellis Street.

So why did George know where the elephant hid? Did Roosevelt want his help? Why did he have that dream?

George wrapped his fingers around a low branch. If he went back to the fairground and told Mel, it could all be over. They could capture Roosevelt and truck him south to rejoin the circus for the next show in Everett. But if it didn't happen there, it would happen further down the line—Roosevelt would try to escape again. The elephant, covered in paint and stars, would just keep trying again and again to be free.

It was warm on the summer streets and warm under the big trees on Commercial Street, and George had time before the movie. During these couple of warm months he owned time, he could do anything he wanted. Was he so lucky he didn't even know? Did he forget all about school that was waiting to start again with the days in class that would herd him inside off his bike away from chasing after and catching dreams? Actually, no…These days were stored, kept in him deep and protected as in a holy ark, a ball of golden summer light in a jar that he would always remember.

He stopped his bicycle and went inside the library where it was quiet and cool and smelled of books and the sunlight was made blue. He ran his hand along the smooth polished card catalogue. He tried to glide on the marble floor.

Sliding his shoes, he was on his way to find out about elephants, but as usual there was an obstacle in his way.

Remus DeWitt doddered before him. The old man, stooped in his overcoat, hadn't noticed the boy yet. It wasn't too late, George thought. Sometimes Remus would catch George and there would go twenty minutes as the old man would tell him about poetry and places he hadn't seen and another world anchored in that old man's memory by cobwebs and creaking wooden wheels. It didn't used to be so bad, Remus could spin a tale like Edgar Rice Burroughs, but since Pearl Harbor a year ago, the old man thought of nothing but the war. He would talk about it for hours until the deep melancholy of his voice would crack from war. He carried the weight of it on him. He shuffled and was bent by the newspaper he carried towards the chair by the fireplace.

George did let him pass without saying hello and maybe that wasn't being polite, maybe the old man needed that boy and his rush of shining summer light the way you open a window for the sound of birds.

It was the second time today George had turned himself invisible…Maybe, he thought, this is what Roosevelt does.

On his sliding, silent feet George ghosted by the checkout counter. He remembered he had two books checked out. He hoped they weren't due. He looked for the librarian he always talked to. The one who gave him *Rootabaga Stories* and the last time he was here, made sure he checked out William Saroyan's *My Name is Aram*. "Read the story in here called The Circus," she told George. It was sitting at home by his bed.

Gliding past the counter, George spun and froze. Distant, sitting under the window at a table with a green lamp was his brother Andrew. There were stacks of books around him and he looked so intent, George didn't dare break his trance. He wanted to. George

91

missed those days of fishing and playing with his brother, but something else was taking place. Better to leave him learning what he had to know.

George skated on towards the shelves of the children's section. When the floor became worn stripes of wood, he walked and followed the grains as they ran him like a string of yarn to the encyclopedias. That was a good place to start with elephants. What did they eat? How *much* did they eat? Where did they like to be?

He found the red leather volume with the gold letter E and he pulled it off the shelf. Turning the pages, he let himself descend until he was sitting on the floor, knees tucked up, back to the shelf. Settling cross-legged, he laid the book on his lap.

Elephants. There was a picture too—a tinted photograph of an African elephant coming out of the tall weeds, its ears held out flat like wings and its trunk raised to blast.

"Elephants eat several hundred pounds of food a day," George read, "Feeding by day and also night."

He knew what Kristine would say to that. He could hear her voice even though she wasn't here. "Jeepers," he whispered.

What could it be? A store with the windows covered in newspaper. What was hiding in there? George stopped and searched for somewhere between all the words and pictures where he might see in. The sheets from the *Herald* were taped on, edge to edge. Whoever did it left an almost perfect job. Just past the scores for the Bells and the Rainiers game, he found a tiny spot missing in the paper. That was all he needed, he could see inside.

Through the little tear in the newsprint, no wider than a penny's edge, George caught a glimpse of a big table inside. One light bulb hung from a cord above, casting its gold like the sun. Below it, across the length and width of the table, was a miniature land. There were mountains, lakes, forest, sea—there was even a train that ran along the shore. *A World At Peace*. He read those words painted on the edge of that world. If he could only get in the store, George thought, he'd love to see it up close.

He didn't get the chance. A big green army truck rumbled up to the stoplight on York Street behind him. It was so loud, George turned around. Across the camouflage siding, a red white and blue banner shouted BUY WAR BONDS. There were cars around it, stopped, idling, looking like a different species. When the light turned, the truck rumbled ahead. It towed a howitzer cannon, aimed back at the *Herald* building.

George watched it go down the street and he wondered why it was here, not overseas, looking for people to kill? Maybe it hadn't been drafted yet? Maybe the truck and its gun didn't get a draft notice and were only seeing the sights, the seashore, the tulip fields, the mountains and lakes. Maybe that truck and its gun would luck out of the war and spend the days peacefully. It could live in the park turned into a statue for the rest of its days, a memorial.

His daydream was interrupted by the slowing of the river of cars in front of him. It was time to cross the street. The pulp mill in the background churned a white cloud above the bay. That's what it did all day, make clouds.

George pushed his bicycle along the white lines of the crosswalk.

On the other side of York, in front of the Grand marquee, George could see Uncle Robert waiting for him. He wore his usual green sweater and porkpie hat, only today he held a wooden chair. You never knew with Uncle Robert. Last week it was a bamboo bird-cage filled with silk ties. When he spotted his nephew, he smiled and freed a hand from the chair to wave.

George returned the wave. He pulled his bike up over the curb and walked it.

"Saint George and his dragon," Uncle Robert greeted him.

"Hello, Uncle Robert."

"Let's see if we can find somewhere to lodge your noble steed. You're going to like this movie, George."

There was a big poster beside the door. Uncle Robert paused and read it dramatically, "They were hounded through 3000 miles of terror! Stealing precious moments of love…stalking a Power they must destroy—or be destroyed! Action—Suspense! As only Director Alfred Hitchcock can portray it! *Saboteur!*"

"How many times have you seen it?"

"So far?" He shifted the chair in his arms. "Ten?" He opened the door, "Roll that bicycle right in here, my good man."

"Hello, Robert," said the uniformed girl in the lobby. Her clothes matched the colors of the elegant room.

"Good afternoon, Dorothy. Could we check my nephew's bicycle for the showing?"

"Of course." She opened the storeroom door, set in the wallpaper between the lobby cards. They had done this before. Everyone knew Robert.

George parked his bicycle beside a mop and a silver bucket. "Thank you," he said.

"You're welcome." Dorothy gave George a pat on the shoulder as he went to join his uncle buying tickets.

Uncle Robert had his coin purse, his chair set by his feet. "One adult, one child," he said.

"Thirty cents."

"Thirty cents," Uncle Robert chuckled. He paid in dimes, adding one more too. "I also need a seat for my chair." He picked it up to show her. "Can you believe it? This was only 88 cents. A brand new chair!"

The girl smiled, "What a bargain!" and gave him three tickets. "Enjoy the movie."

They could feel the hum of it already, the music and murmurs as they followed the hallway.

"Can we sit in the balcony?" George asked.

"You read my mind."

Up the spiraling stairs, through the swinging door with its round portal of glass, they entered the huge theater room. George marveled at the stream of white light projected from the bright window in back, a smoky rivering overhead that ended painting the screen far below.

In the dark, the seats climbed a slant. There were only a few other people up here.

George pointed. "Is this a good spot?"

Uncle Robert said, "Perfect." They sat down and Robert turned his chair and placed it on the seat next to him, its four feet kicked in the air.

George rocked his plush seat back and forth a
little. Over the drop of the balcony, there were more
people dotted in the rounded backs of chairs. On the
big screen was a newsreel. Thick black smoke rolled
out of a burning battleship. The announcer promised
it would never happen again. An American flag was
waving.

"Uncle Robert," George whispered, "What do you
think will happen to that elephant?"

"The one that escaped?"

"Yeah. I don't think he wants to go back to the
circus."

"Hmmm," said Uncle Robert. "You're probably
right."

The room turned silver as the credits rolled, as
that battleship and all those dead sailors turned to mist
on the ceiling of the Grand Theatre in 1942. From either side the big red curtains shuffled across the screen,
meeting in the middle, swimming together.

"What if I found the elephant?" said George. "Is
there somewhere he could go that wasn't a circus or a
zoo, where there were other elephants too?"

"Hmmm," said Uncle Robert. "There is...If you
found the elephant, there is a way."

All at once the curtains began to part again, clacking and swishing and the Universal Pictures music and
spinning world appeared on the screen, stars twinkling
and turning on shafts of white light.

Then George was staring at a wall of corrugated metal. It reminded him of the night they saw the circus, the dark industrial lots by the fairground. An ominous looking shadow man began to creep while all the titles and words came and went. The silhouette on the screen grew closer and closer.

George held the ten dollar bill, staring as if it was the feather off a rare bird.

"Go ahead," Uncle Robert said, "Put that in your pocket. Go to the market and get as much elephant food as you can."

George folded the money quickly and pushed it into his pocket. On the street around him he pictured gangs of bank robbers watching him. He hopped up onto his bicycle.

"Good luck," Uncle Robert said. He stood there in front of the theater surrounded by neon and blinking yellow light bulbs that clung to the edges of the Grand. Above him on the marquee the black letters spelled *Saboteur*, the movie he was going back in to watch again. It played over and over into night. He could get his fill. Tomorrow a new movie began. The movie palace days seemed to never end. He saluted George as the boy crossed the street and waved at his uncle, then disappeared with the traffic down Commercial.

George actually stopped under a shady red Japanese maple tree, and after looking down the sidewalk way he had come and the path ahead, he looked at that ten dollar bill again. It felt real, though he never held one before. A ten spot, a real sawbuck! He tried to imagine how much elephant food that would buy... Enough to fill a wheelbarrow, he supposed. He would need help. He returned the folded money to his pocket and pedaled for Girard Street.

George knew all the shortcuts in town. There wasn't an alley he didn't know. In his mind he had the Top Secret Map, directions that would make him seem to disappear like Geronimo, parting azaleas and overhanging ivy, to slip through fences, paths shared with animals, cats and dogs and deer, he could pop up on a different block as if he had tunneled underground or caught a ride on a bird.

He thought about the movie. He loved the part with the circus, when the trucks arrived across the nighttime desert, headlights shining off the screen in rays right into his eyes. He wished he too could have hopped onto that last truck and met those circus performers inside—the sleepy fat lady, the eloquent ringmaster who spoke like Remus DeWitt, the kindly bearded lady who saw their innocence, even the mean dwarf who tried to rat them out.

George thought about Mel Tell out there on the fairground. Was he just sitting at that little table with his clown shoes kicked up, waiting for Roosevelt to show? George looked up when he heard a buzzing airplane and wondered if the clown was standing on the wing, searching the countryside, holding tight against the wind?

The dandelions all over Kristine's lawn made him think of her freckles. He set his bicycle on the same red steps as last night.

This wouldn't be his first animal adventure with Kristine. There was the time just after the Berlin zoo got bombed. There was an awful photo in the *Herald* of a dead giraffe. George and Kristine happened to be riding their bikes down Bay Street and they saw a man emptying buckets in the sea. He had seen the newspaper too and he didn't want the aquarium to end up that way. They helped him put every creature back where it came from.

"Hi, George."

He shaded his eyes. Kristine was standing in the glare of sunlight, watering the flowers along the edge of the house. She held a watering can. Best of all though, she had a wagon parked beside her. There was plenty of room in that wagon. It looked like it could hold ten dollars worth of food.

"What are you doing?" she asked.

"I'm going to see the circus elephant. Do you

want to come?"

Her eyes went wide as clovers.

"My father wanted to give this wagon to the scrap drive," Kristine said. Its wheels made a fine soft thumping on each crack of sidewalk. "But I wouldn't let him. I've had this wagon since I learned to walk."

"It's a good one alright. I bet we can fill it really high."

"Do you really think we'll find Roosevelt?"

"I'm sure of it. I saw him in my dream last night." George lowered his voice, "He's in the creek. He's hiding in the trees." George switched the wagon handle to his other hand. It had been a long time since he pulled a wagon. Also, he felt a little out of sorts walking instead of riding his faithful bicycle. He left the bike at Kristine's. He couldn't push it through a grocery store or down the steep track into the creek ravine.

There were corner stores in every neighborhood. Even down the alley at George's house was a garage called The Bungalow Dairy, the perfect place to buy a stick of butter or get a couple extra eggs for breakfast. But with ten dollars and an elephant to feed, they needed somewhere bigger.

The Safeway on Dupont…

George knew what his mother would say. She would be appalled. Their family had been shopping at their neighborhood market for far longer than George had been alive. They were known there like family, they bought on account there. Sometimes when George felt daring, he would bring candy to the counter and say, "Put it on our account." The shopkeeper would give him the eye, "Do you have permission?" George couldn't promise he did. But on his birthday they always gave him a bag of licorice.

So George was nervous as they rolled the wagon into the Safeway parking lot. He scanned the cars and the people going in and out. A crow hopped ahead of them then took flight.

"I've never been here before," he mumbled.

"Really?" Kristine said. "We go here all the time. They have the cheapest prices."

A banner stretched across the windows, 27th Anniversary Sale! There were sale signs taped over every inch of the glass. It was a wonder they even bothered with windows.

"We need to get vegetables and fruit," said George. "That's what elephants like."

He followed Kristine into the Safeway. Pulling the wagon past the checkout aisles, there were rows of food in tins and bags and paper boxes. The place seemed to go on and on. He was glad she knew the way. He couldn't believe how much food there was. He imagined what someone from the other side of the globe, from a bombed-out city struggling for life would think, walking in here, looking around. Or, he thought, instead of bombs, couldn't we fill those B-17s

104

with all this food? Dropped by parachute of course…
But that wouldn't be war, would it? War was for killing
all those people on the ground. Nobody was meant to
live. We weren't supposed to help anyone until afterwards, if anyone survived.

George wasn't really watching where he was going.
He was adrift like a balloon and the wagon seemed to
glide on the waxy floor and there was music drifting
out of hidden speakers, or did it just live on the air in
here? "There'll be bluebirds over the White Cliffs of
Dover," some voice was singing with orchestra. George
felt hypnotized until the wagon knocked a can of tomatoes off the shelf he floated by. "Oh!"

He hurried to put it back with the silvery row of
the rest of them. His face felt flush as the red picture
on the can. Then he grabbed the handle and hurried
on, though carefully, after Kristine. Only a yard from
the cans of tomatoes were shiny jars of peppers for
sale. He was glad he didn't knock one of them down.

At the end of the aisle, Kristine turned to the left
and stopped. There was a wooden bin, filled with wa-
termelons, green as jade and smooth as river stones.

"What do you think?" she smiled. "They're four
cents a pound."

"Perfect." Then George got close to her red hair to
whisper, "I don't think we should mention we're shopping for an elephant."

She nodded. "It's for a picnic," she whispered
back.

105

"The only thing is, we have to keep track of how much we're buying. We can't run over ten dollars."

Kristine had a handbag she wore on a long braided rope over her shoulder. It was just big enough to hold her sketchbook and some pens. Embroidered on the side was a cloth flower she made and sewed on. She took out the sketchbook and a pencil and found an empty page. She wrote 10.00 at the top.

"Oh no," said George. "We have to do math."

"Don't worry." She picked up a watermelon and set it on the scale. They watched the needle jitter and stick. "Five pounds. It costs four cents a pound…Four times five is twenty. Twenty cents."

George lifted the fruit off the scale and put it in the wagon. "Let's get a few of them."

"Okay," she said. She started writing numbers in the book. Next it was lemons, a dozen for 15¢. Apples were 8¢ a pound. They piled on carrots at four bunches for a dime. Yams and potatoes, Kristine added them up. A head of lettuce cost a nickel. They could get a lot. Cucumbers were 10¢ each, so maybe just two.

When Kristine figured there was about enough, George found three celery stalks that he stuck in the peak of the wagonful of food so it looked like a giant cake with candles.

Now that George was carrying such a heavy, precious cargo he steered and pulled the wagon like a captain at sea. Kristine walked beside the freight of vegetables and fruit, catching a yellow apple from tumbling.

As they cleared the aisle, George switched the handle to the right hand and paused beside the tall humming cooler. "Do you think we still have enough money for a RC cola?"

Kristine looked pensive, pursed her lips and said, "Maybe just one."

George opened the cold lid and grabbed a bottle. The icy steam went up his sleeve.

It would take both hands to get the wagon started again. "You better carry this," he said and passed her the Royal Crown.

"Gee, it's cold!"

George had to laugh for a second. "It'll taste good when we're out in that hot sun again." He tugged the boatload of produce to the cashier and stopped in line.

The person in front of them paying for a bag of rice looked back in surprise.

The cashier took one look at their wagon and she said, "Is this more elephant bait?"

"Oh no," said George quickly.

"A lot of people are out trying to catch Roosevelt today."

Kristine told her, "We're going to a picnic."

The cashier shook her head and sighed. "Alright, well, let's count it up."

They did have enough for the Royal Crown soda. And a few coins to spare. Maybe they could have bought another lettuce, but they couldn't have fit it in the wagon.

The afternoon heat baked the sidewalk. It seemed cooked and crisp as a bumpy sheet-cake. George tried to take care and go slow but sometimes some round fruit or vegetable would roll off the pile.

They were on York Street, about a street away from the creek, the only problem being George wasn't exactly sure where the elephant was in the ravine. His dream wasn't that specific. The creek stringed its way four miles from the bay to the big lake it branched off from. George knew he would just have to sense the place. He would know where the elephant was the way a dowser felt the presence of water. Cars were passing them, it didn't seem like home to an elephant, yet George believed it was time to try the ravine.

They made it across the street and up onto the next curb where the trees lined and overhung and the cooling drop into leafy shadows could be felt like an oasis underlying the hot city. The woods were so thick it looked like a dragon could hide right here in the heart of town and nobody would know it was around.

Kristine gave him a quick look. She didn't say

anything, she didn't need to.

"We're almost there," he said. And then he remembered Billy Van Sloat and his Japanese airplane that wasn't there, and he prayed this wouldn't be like that. There had to be an elephant, Roosevelt had to be waiting for them. The road began to veer from the nearness of the creek, pulling the sidewalk along with it, leaving behind a vacant lot full of weeds along the embankment.

This was where George chose to pull the front wheels off the cement and with Kristine's help guide the wagon onto unpaved terrain. Right away they lost a head of lettuce overboard. George stopped while Kristine picked it up and dusted the torn leaf. She put it back on but it was plain to see that was only the beginning. The bumpy ground was knotted and burred with weeds and stones, crowded with Queen Anne's lace and yarrow. Kristine kept both her hands hovering over the wagon load. George pulled slow and tried his best.

It reminded him of the Larrisons who lived on E Street. These summer days they sat outside on the front porch and whenever George had the time he would stop and say hello. They were so old they came here in a covered wagon. They told George about seeing the buffalo on the plains. Once Mr. Larrison showed George the Conestoga wheel they still kept, the only thing left from that wooden contraption that time traveled them here.

George imagined Kristine and him, old as the Larrisons, living in a little house under a tall tree with only a red wagon wheel to recall the trial of this day's long journey. George pointed and said, "Let's stop under that tree."

They didn't make it there without a casualty. Kristine gave a shriek as a cantaloupe fell and hit the ground. It was inevitable though really. How could they make it across the prairie without some adversity? George pulled the wagon under the syrupy leaves of a tall willow tree and found a good place to park where it was level and hidden by brush.

Nearby there was a narrow trail that switchbacked twice down to the creek. Now they were away from the traffic they could actually hear the water flow.

Kristine stood at the steep edge in the ironweed and spindly wildflowers. Through the canopy of green below there was a tiny window between some leaves that showed the sparkling creek. From behind her came the unmistakable crisp crunching sound of an apple bite. She spun and stared at George, a red apple in his hand.

"George!"

"Sorry…I'm hungry."

"That's Roosevelt's food!"

"I know. It feels like we walked across Kansas though. I'm sure he wouldn't mind sharing an apple or two. Do you want one?" He took another bite.

"No thank you." She started out on the trail and George hurried to catch up. He carried a cantaloupe tucked under his arm like a football.

It was as if they had gone below the city, excavated through the levels of cellars and water mains, gone past the old coal mines into the geology of some other long ago time. It was quiet and peaceful, only the marmalade color of the stream, the sound of its chirping water, a dipper hopping along the stony edge, fluttering its wings. It felt slow down here, only the shimmer of the water, all the trees, and the elephant.

Roosevelt stood not more than fifty feet from them in a thick paddy of ferns. He watched them stop and stare. He lifted his trunk and breathed. Whatever it was he drew in from them gave him no reason to be alarmed. He stood there peacefully.

"Jeepers," George gasped. He whispered, "It's Roosevelt…" He flicked the apple core off into the snowberry and salal and held the cantaloupe with both hands. "Should we try to feed him?"

"I think so," Kristine whispered.

George took a step closer to the elephant. He held the cantaloupe out in front of him.

Kristine crept along beside him.

"Can you believe it's really him?" George grinned.

"No…"

Roosevelt gave a flap of his big ears.

George purred, "Easy, Roosevelt. We're your

113

friends. You can tell, right? We brought you a bunch of food."

They were close now. There was a deep rumbling coming from Roosevelt like, George thought, the Philco radio when you first turned it on and the dial would begin to glow.

George stuck his arms out as far as they would go, offering the cantaloupe. The twigs crunched beneath their feet and the ferns rubbed their legs.

Roosevelt lifted his trunk again and snaked it out to the fruit.

George held his breath as the trunk wrapped around the melon and plucked it out of his hands.

So gently it didn't even crush the rind, the elephant popped the cantaloupe into his mouth like a grape.

Kristine squeezed George's arm. "He ate it!" she whispered.

"Would you like more, Roosevelt?" George asked.

"We have a whole wagon full," said Kristine, finding her voice.

Roosevelt held out his trunk again.

"Come on, Kristine. We have to carry all that food down here." They were so excited they were practically singing, flying like birds out of the ravine.

At first they carried the food down the hill in George's jacket, held between them like a hammock and then finally they rattled the wagon into the ravine and what was left rolled around.

The elephant ate everything they gave him.

Coming all the way to find him, talking to him, and feeding him was all they needed to do to gain Roosevelt's trust. He even let them close to pet him. His skin was like the bark of one of the trees he stood among. Kristine said she wished she had brought her paint. "I could have put some stars on him." She was happy though to see up close how there were lines going all over him, connecting him like thousands of pencils had drawn him into existence.

"Sorry, Roosevelt," George told the elephant, "That's all the food we have." He said to Kristine, "I guess we better go."

"I know." She patted Roosevelt. "We have to go home, Roosevelt."

They left him there, an elephant tucked in among the blooms of ocean spray and tall thorny stalks of devil's club. They hopped across the stones in the creek. The water striders danced away from them, skating across the reflected forest.

Kristine and George had been in another world, one of timeless woods and creatures, but when they came back to the vacant lot, they were in 1942.

Five warplanes in formation roared low overhead.

Kristine cupped her ears and George shouted, "P-38s!" In the scouts they had to learn all the planes.

The aircraft shot across the city and banked tightly, black dots the sunlight glinted on, twisting their wings over the tall spire of the city hall. George said, "Those are fighter planes."

"What are they doing?" She still had her hands bunched in her red hair. "Are they Japanese?"

"No. They're ours." George dropped the wagon handle and put his hand on his brow to shade his eyes. "I lost them…" There were thick white clouds out over the islands. "We better get home."

"I hope nothing happened."

The wagon wheels clattered over the sort of pasture for weeds. Above them, dragonflies zigged and zagged. It was hot away from the creek, the trees, shading a camouflaged elephant.

As George pulled the wagon onto the sidewalk, pulling it was suddenly a lot easier.

A green army car drove by on the street. As it growled away, they heard "George!" yelled from behind them, not far. "George!"

He and Kristine saw who it was. Billy Van Sloat and his older brother ran towards them in nothing short of a panic. They both jumped and turned at the bland looking car that passed them.

"George…" Billy panted. "Hey…Kristine…Did you see the plane?"

"Those P-38s?"

"No!" Billy twisted his neck to wipe his face on the shoulder of his shirt. He and his brother were both shining with sweat. "The plane before them…"

"Come on, Billy," his brother punched Billy's arm. "We gotta hide!"

"What for?" George asked.

"That's what I'm trying to tell you," Billy said. He rubbed his sore arm. "Remember the model airplane contest?"

George nodded.

"We made a German bomber and flew it."

"Radio control," said Billy's brother. He took off his wire rim glasses and used a handkerchief on his face.

"Right over town!" Billy held out his hands, "Back and forth."

"Three times that we saw," added Billy's brother.

"Before we had to scram," Billy broke in.

Billy's brother continued, "Once it reached altitude, I set the controls so it would fly in a circling bomber formation." He still seemed edgy but not in so much of a rush to tarnish his achievement. George was reminded of those villains in the crime movies who always had to boast to the hero how cunning they were. Meanwhile the hero would be untying his ropes.

"It's crazy!" Billy said. "The whole city went crazy. I don't know how you missed it, George. Now those army planes are out looking for the Luftwaffe!"

Another car passed them and Billy's brother grabbed him. "We have to lay low. Word might have got around." He tugged Billy off the edge of cement onto the field George and Kristine just left. "Come on!" They started to wade in.

George dropped the wagon handle with a clack. "No!" he shouted. "You can't go in the ravine. That's where we were. It's crawling with cops!"

"What?" The two brothers looked wild-eyed at the creek treetops.

"Yeah! We didn't know what they were doing."

"Okay, okay." Billy's brother pointed across the street. "Let's go that way." He pulled his brother's damp sleeve.

"Thanks, George," Billy called back. The two of them ran like fugitives across the hot tar. There were alleys on the other side of the road, garages and loading docks and hiding places behind chain link fence.

"Wow..." George sighed.

When they were out of sight, Kristine smiled and said, "It's crawling with cops!" a near perfect imitation of him. She touched him and laughed.

"Yeah, yeah," he said and kicked a pebble out into the street.

How did George and Kristine miss all the commotion? The same way the elephant did, by disappearing into a hidden world, going invisible to danger.

Only an hour ago at the high school auditorium, tables were set up across the gleaming wooden floor of the gym. City officials, the Mayor and Army Air Corp officers, children, parents, a news reporter from the *Herald*—they were all examining and admiring the many airplane models for the contest. There were trophies, ribbons and those big dollar prizes awaiting the end of the judging. The Mayor had his people making notes and talking, he was just waiting, smoking a cigarette, giving them time with the paperwork.

Someone, one of the younger kids who stayed outside on the playground, came running inside telling everyone to hurry out, to see what was flying past. The boy was in such a panic, they did, expecting to see a pterodactyl carrying off the Mayor's Chrysler.

They crowded around the boy outside where he jumped and pointed and they all saw it too. There was no doubt about it. They had seen them on the newsreels, over Spain, Poland, and the London blitz: A Heinkel 111 bomber.

The Air Raid Warden, an old man who wore his white metal doughboy hat and uniform, raised his trembling binoculars to catch hold of the sight of it. His voice rasped out a squawk of alarm for there on those crow-shaped wings was something he thought he'd never see—black and white crosses. Everyone on the edge of the playground buzzed and shook each other in a commotion of rising terror.

As the bomber slid behind the cover of cottonwood trees, the Mayor took a deep breath, held up his hands and quieted the crowd, reminded them it was everyone's patriotic duty to stay calm. He was sure the armed forces were aware of the situation—this was no Pearl Harbor. The mayor knew he had to inspire confidence and this was his moment to shine. He took a deep breath, set his jaw grimly and was about to begin a stirring speech when the Air Warden screeched, "It's coming back!"

There was a collective scream and everyone was bumping into each other, falling and running and scattering.

All that pandemonium that began not even a mile away, that spread out across town like a stone thrown into a pond…there was no way Kristine and George and the elephant Roosevelt could have know that was going on. They were far from that civilization in a green dream of trees and slow moving water.

At Kristine's house, George finally let go of the wagon. He laughed and showed her how his hand was bent into a claw from holding it so long. He pretended he was some Boris Karloff maniac and cupped it over Kristine's shoulder.

Alerted by their laughing, Kristine's mother came to the porch and called, "Kristine! It's time for dinner."

"Alright." She put a last clawed hand on George and pulled it away. She said quietly, "Can we go see Roosevelt again tomorrow?"

"Sure. Only that's the last of my money. Maybe we could just say hi to him."

"Look," she said. She pulled the RC cola bottle from her bag. "We forgot about this."

"That's okay," George said. "Keep it. Save it for someday a long time from now. Save it like one of those fancy wine bottles. The bottle of Elephant, 1942."

She laughed.

"Kristine!" her mother called her again.

"Okay!"

"Well, I'll see you then," George said. He got his bicycle. It had spent the long day with hers.

George rode across the chalked hopscotch games left like bright patchwork farms on the sidewalk. He slowed upon one, with his shadow hung over it like a windmill and gave the marker stone a little kick. He remembered this game, though it had been a long time since he played. He also hadn't pulled a wagon in years until today so he supposed you never really know when old things would find you again.

He pedaled across the rest of the numbers and lines, watched the hopscotch end in a garden of scribbled pictures. There was a yellow sun and flowers, a trolley or a train, airplanes and even an elephant. He could tell this was a story someone took time to make and leave on the cement when they went inside for dinner.

At Liberty Park he slowed down again. Something was going on. Two big touring buses were parked at the curb, elm trees overhead like umbrellas. Along the silvery panel of one of the buses was painted Morgan Russman Orchestra.

A man was unloading a drum set from the big cargo hatch. He made a broad wave at George. There were other musicians too, some of them carrying their instruments. They were converging on the bandstand, across the wide lawn with its sprinkling of dandelions and early evening shadows.

Someone was sitting on a park bench along the path, playing a trumpet, the horn tone as yellow and orange as a Fall wind on the way. Even from a distance, George could tell who it was; the sound was as distinct to the boy on the bench as the call of some morning bird.

Cornelius Barter in age was somewhere between George and Andrew. He was a sort of mystery though, a loner who carried his trumpet case everywhere he went, popping it open to play in empty trolley cars, or alleys where the walls echoed away like an Egyptian mosque call to prayer.

George only knew him as the boy with the trumpet. And there he was—that pearly tone playing for the Russman Orchestra. As they passed him, some of them said something, some would snap their fingers or cheer him some way, and another trumpet player sat down and took out his horn and joined in.

"Evening, son."

A man in a blue suit stood next to George. He held a trombone so shiny it looked like a lightning bolt.

"Hello, sir."

"Sir! I like that." The man smiled. "I'm Morgan Russman. You hear about the big dance tonight?"

"No, sir. I was just riding by."

"You do much dancing, son?"

"Oh, no, I guess not."

"That's alright." Morgan Russman laughed. "Here," he said. He took a hand off that trombone and reached in his pocket, taking out two tickets. "Why don't you give these to someone who does?"

George held the crisp tickets in his hand, read the beautiful print on them, Morgan Russman and his Melodious Dance Orchestra! There were little music notes flying from a trombone, all around the paper like birds. "Thank you."

"Do you play an instrument?"

George paused a second. He put the tickets in his coat pocket and said, "I have this—"

Morgan Russman turned the wooden horn around in his fingers. "What's it do?"

"It's an elephant caller."

"An elephant caller!"

"Yes, sir. Only please don't try it out. I don't want to disturb the elephant."

Morgan Russman chuckled. "I won't," he promised and passed it back to George. "Let sleeping elephants lie, that's what I always say."

"Yes, sir," George nodded solemnly.

The trombonist laughed. "Well, I have to get going, son. We've got a show to get ready for."

Behind him, across all the grass, Cornelius Barter had gathered his first jazz band.

It made it by the tall row of telephone poles on Cornwall, the wires glinting with sun, but it hit a poplar tree and went down smoking into the playfield corner of Washington elementary school. The Heinkel 111 scudded to a landing in the dirt.

The Van Sloat brothers had made a dreadful work of art. Their plane lay there looking exactly like it had been brought down by Spitfires. A crew of miniature Germans could have come stumbling out, surrendering.

It didn't take long before the schoolyard was surrounded by police cars, green military vehicles, the old Air Raid Warden and his crew of volunteers. From behind sandbags, they viewed the crashed bomber with binoculars. The Nazi plane with its bent propellers, cracked glass nacelle and trail of shattered fuselage and wings lay unmoving in the dirt. Someone needed to venture out across that open ground.

The Mayor arrived and shook hands with the Commanding Officer. He spoke with the bomb squad and watched them crouch towards the plane. Or maybe, he supposed aloud to his aides, it wasn't exactly a plane—it was of course too small for a pilot to fit inside—maybe, it was some dastardly new invention, a flying camera launched by U-Boat submarine, or even worse, a high explosive, ticking flying bomb.

By the time the soldiers reached the plane, the Mayor held his hands tight over his ears, sure that an explosion was about to occur. One of his assistants had to tap him and tell him it was okay. It was only a model.

The Mayor stood up, brushed the dirt off his knees, and could see the men carrying the broken plane between them. It was empty inside, run out of fuel, and dangling a wheel like the foot of a dead heron. Only a model plane! Yes, maybe this time, the Mayor told them. They were lucky this time. Actually, he went on, this had been an opportunity to test their preparedness for such an event. And they were found woefully lacking! What they needed was a controlled test, he said. Even if this small town, with its paper mill, railyards, banks and commerce may seem of little consequence, big things could happen here. He took a breath and told the men around him, "Tomorrow night we need to show Uncle Sam that we're pre-pared."

It had been a long busy day. George had his soup and ate six ears of corn on the cob. He felt like Roosevelt. He didn't tell his parents about the elephant though. He didn't need to; the German plane was all anyone could talk about. When they did get around to where he'd been, he showed his parents the tickets for Morgan Russman. That was like handing his mother a big bouquet. He didn't expect her reaction though he knew how she loved the music on the radio. That was an hour ago.

When they were ready to go, they found George asleep on the couch. He didn't even know when his father picked him up and carried him past Andrew, reading by the radio, down the hallway to his bedroom. He smelled his mother's perfume as she bent over him, changing his clothes into pajamas.

His eyes sort of opened to the dark room, the silhouettes of his parents whispering goodnight. George was so tired he might have said elephant, so sleepy he might have thought he was at the creek again, with a blanket of leaves and ferns pulled over him, murmuring goodnight, goodnight.

Not quite. The summer breeze pushed the curtains inwards and poured music carried from Liberty Park. It sounded like the orchestra was up in the trees, glowing like colored paper lanterns. Enough to wake George, opening his eyes to see if candlelight danced on his ceiling and walls and thinking of his parents over there holding onto each other like the lovers on a movie screen while the big band played them and all the rest of the moms and dads back and forth on the lawn and dandelions as he closed his eyes and fell back to sleep.

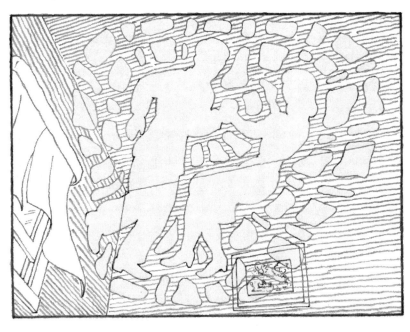

In the morning a new sound drove through the chirping birds, the radios and breakfast chores. It was a truck with speakers on the roof pointed like big flowers at the houses going slowly by. *"The city will be conducting an air raid drill tonight at 9 PM."* The truck rolled on past the windows and porches, hedges and driveways, inching along, repeating its message on down the street.

"What's that all about?" said George with his hands on the glass. He lost sight of the strange looking truck behind a rhododendron.

"There's going to be a black-out tonight." His mother said, "They're going to turn off all the lights downtown. We have to cover our windows and wait for the all-clear signal." She wrapped her arms around George and held him tight enough to feel his breath and heartbeat.

The truck faded away, returned the neighborhood to the birds and radios and sounds of chores. Also another sound George could feel trembling from his mother as she held him—she was crying. He felt a tear on his neck and she kissed the top of his head and let him go. She covered her eyes with the back of her hand and hurried from the room.

George stayed at the window, looking out. The

street was still. Only when the house was really quiet could you hear the clock ticking on the mantel.

His brother walked into view and George rapped on the glass.

Andrew turned in surprise. He waved when he saw the boy watching him, then he motioned for him to come outside.

George ran to put on his shoes and pushed the front door open. The milk truck rattled past on the street. George shut the door and leaped with his arms out flying. "Hey!" he said as he slowed on the grass and shoved his hands in his pockets.

Andrew grinned. "Hey, George." He pointed and walked around the back of the house with the boy following. George tried out walking in those same big steps.

Andrew stopped by the garden shed. "Can I borrow your bike today?"

"My bike? What happened to yours?"

"I sold it."

"Why?"

"I won't need it anymore. Didn't Mom and Dad tell you? I'm being inducted tomorrow. The army wants me. They've got their own train that comes through town and takes us away."

George stared at Andrew. He was looking at his brother today, right now, but he was already seeing him disappear.

Andrew patted George's shoulder and smiled.

"Listen, there's still some things I have to get. If I can use your bike it would save me some time."

"Alright."

"Yeah?"

George nodded.

"Thanks, George." Andrew opened the shed.

"Hey, I'll get you some licorice or something." He took the bicycle out and stood it beside him. It looked small for him. "I'll see you, George."

"Okay," George said, watching him start to pedal and wobble and laugh and leave. "See you."

So he walked to Kristine's. It wasn't far but he did miss his bike. The sidewalk wasn't so fast.

He walked around the flowered side of her house and sure enough, she was on the porch, painting a picture.

"Hi," he called.

"Hi."

"You painting another elephant?"

She made a face at him. "Yes…" Then she set her brush down and came over to the screen window to whisper. "Can we go see Roosevelt again?"

George nodded. "Only…I've been thinking… What if we helped him to get away?"

Kristine slipped out the screen door. "How?"

"My Uncle Robert will help."

"Really? Has he caught elephants before?"

"Not that I know of…But I wouldn't be surprised."

"Okay. Let me get my bag and we can go see your uncle." She went back on the porch with George following her.

"Well…" he said. "I'm not exactly sure where my uncle will be."

"Doesn't he have a home?"

"Yes…But during the day he goes to the movies."

"Oh…What time do the movies start?"

"The matinee is at one-ish."

Kristine dropped the paintbrush in its jar of water. "One-ish? Why do people always say ish?"

"I don't know."

"One-ish, two-ish. Green-ish, blue-ish." She put her bag over her shoulder. She sighed dramatically.

George was thinking though. He couldn't wait for her birthday party. He would write 'Happy Birthday-ish' in her card.

"Do we know which theater he will go to?"

"Ummm…" George said.

"Let's bring the newspaper with us."

"Good idea," George said.

Kristine took the paper off the rocking chair. She turned the pages to the middle and found where the movies were listed. "Did you read Popeye today?"

George shook his head.

"It's pretty funny." She pulled that section free from the *Herald*, folding it to fit in her bag. "We can look at this when we get downtown."

They left the cool shaded porch and jumped down the wooden steps to the yard.

"Where's your bicycle?"

George told her, "My brother needed it. We'll have to walk."

"Okay." While they did, she took the newspaper out of her bag. "Here," she said, "Read Popeye to me. Make sure you read it in his voice though."

"I'll try."

Kristine held the newspaper. George marveled at how the freckles on her hand seemed to run off onto the page and turn into words. Or was it the other way around? Maybe he could read her skin, those dots a part of an alphabet he hadn't yet learned.

A few blocks from them, up Holly Street, the Peoples Theatre was showing a Charlie Chan movie in the evening. The American had two Westerns, but no matinee. The Avalon had Abbott and Costello, a possibility if Uncle Robert needed a laugh. Anyway, George wanted to see it.

"We went to the Grand yesterday." George tapped the page next to her thumb. "Look at this though… The Mount Baker, starting today, *Moontide*. This has to be the one."

Kristine leaned closer to read it, one silky red hair, fine as the thread from a spider web tickled George's face. Above the picture of Ida Lupino looking cool as a silky mermaid, Kristine read, "Men. I know them all and I hate 'em all." Her voice quickly moved to Brooklyn as she continued. "Then this Longshoreman came along. One look and it's like I never seen a guy before. He's tough. He lives too fast. He's dangerous to love. But I can't sleep for thinkin' of bein' in his arms."

George leaped in with a radio announcer voice, to

finish reading the ad, "Shocking! Daring! Thrilling! A powerful drama that will live in your memory forever."

They both laughed.

"Oh yeah," George said. "Uncle Robert is definitely there."

A trolley rang its bell as it passed them. George saw the driver raise his blue uniform arm. "That's my Dad!" George and Kristine waved back to the trolley. Blue sparks of Frankenstein electricity crackled off the wires above it as it turned with the cars.

George and Kristine also turned, towards the steeple-looking tower that rose above the street. In red letters climbing down from the tiled roof, the tower read Mt. Baker.

There were white posters lining the street tacked on the telephone poles, thick black letters that said, *The City Will Be Conducting an Air Raid Drill Tonight at 9 PM.*

Two sparrows chased each other into the hawthorn tree above the sidewalk.

"George…" Kristine said, "I don't have any money, do you? How will we get in?"

"Oh…" George slowed and dug into his pocket. There was still the change from Safeway. He spread it about on his palm. "We have eight cents."

"How much is a ticket?"

"It's ten, I think."

"Oh dear."

"Well…Let's just see what happens. Maybe they'll

138

let us in, just to see my uncle." They crossed the street.

Moontide Starts Today filled the marquee, surrounded by flickering light bulbs. Below, a girl in a red uniform sat at the ticket booth window.

Kristine touched George's shoulder to give him good luck.

"Hello," he said. He put his hands on the slick marble window ledge and talked into the hole cut in the glass. "We need to see my uncle. He's inside watching the movie. Can we get him and come back out?"

"The picture's already started," said the girl. "We don't like to disturb the other patrons."

"I know. I'm sorry. It's urgent."

"His uncle's wife is having a baby," Kristine told her.

"Oh," said the girl. "Let me get an usher." She stood up and turned around and opened the door at the back of the booth. They watched her go, her red dress, gold braiding and clicking shoes, to the glass entrance doors. "I'll be right back."

"Jeepers, Kristine!" George hissed. "What'd you say that for?"

She laughed and said, "I don't know! It just popped in my head. I think I saw that happen in a movie. Anyway, it worked. She's going to get us an usher. Look—"

The girl held the door open for them. An usher, a boy with a flashlight, stood waiting in the lobby. He waved.

"You can come in," said the girl.

"Good night!…" whispered George. "Here we go."

George said they should try the balcony and up the stairs they went, following the usher. It did feel like they were being led inside a castle—the red carpet was woven with Arabic designs, the wide stairway climbed past the height of the chandeliers in the lobby. Everything was gold and red and twinkling as the center of some precious jewel.

At the top floor, the usher led them to the balcony door, switching on his flashlight so a crystal ball danced in front of them.

As they entered the darkness, Kristine grabbed George's hand.

Over the edge of the balcony, projected on the wall below, a little boat rowed across the screen, the background full of fog and a seawall with gulls watching and shadows in flight.

The music glided them up to a bait shack where the man with the oars reached out and stopped them and stepped out. "Alright now," the sailor said. "Come on." He reached into the stern and pulled a girl off the lap of the man holding her.

She asked, "Where are you taking me?"

He said, "You're okay, you're okay. Take it easy."

George spotted Uncle Robert without too much trouble. How many people wear a top hat to see a

141

movie?

The usher stood in the aisle while George and Kristine scurried down the row.

"George?" Uncle Robert whispered.

The movie music got louder and George had to wait until they were next to Uncle Robert. Beside him, George sat in a plush chair with Kristine sinking into her own.

"Uncle Robert. I do know where the elephant is. We saw him yesterday. But I don't think he can hide very long where he is."

"Woah, woah."

"You said you would help him."

"I know…" Uncle Robert sighed. "Okay, let me think for a second." He clasped his hands and held them, praying, before his face and closed his eyes.

He gave them time to watch the movie.

It was hard to ignore. The people were large as giants, their voices filled the room.

The lady stepped out of the fish shack wearing a dress. The music was playing violins and muted brass like a lullaby.

"I'm blowing now," she said.

"Oh yeah?" the sailor said.

"Yeah." She reached and shook his hand. "Well, I'm much obliged for everything."

He laughed a little. "Ah, it's nothing." The smoke from his cigarette clouded about. "What are you going to do now?"

"Pick up where I left off. Find something to do. I'm okay now." She smiled.

"Well, so long."

Her eyes sparkled. "Thanks again. She crossed the wooden slats and he followed to watch her leave up the steep stairs to the dock.

"Good luck, Sunny Side," he said.

The sweet music played and Uncle Robert brought his praying hands down. "Okay," he said. "I'll help you."

In his top hat he looked like a magician, with the two children skipping along beside him as if the backstreets and alleys were the carefully penned out route to a pirate's treasure. Really though, their excited laughter was taking them towards an elephant.

Uncle Robert shook his head in astonishment. "You told them my wife is having a baby?"

Kristine giggled.

"That was her idea," George said.

"You've given me an imaginary family, Kristine." Uncle Robert smiled. "What do you think I should tell them when I go back later to finish seeing the movie?"

George sighed, "Oh boy."

"Yes," Kristine chirped. "Tell them it's a boy—no wait! Tell them you have twins!"

"Twins!"

Kristine was laughing again.

"Alright. I'll say I have twins. A boy named George and a girl named Kristine."

They laughed and walked into a dirt alley behind Kansas Street. A spring mattress slumped against the back of an old carriage house. Ivy grew in twines among the rust. Sleeping Beauty had turned into foxglove and buttercups.

"Can you really help Roosevelt get somewhere

safe?" George asked.

Uncle Robert said, "I'll try my best. An elephant's pretty big though."

"Where are you going to hide him?" Kristine asked.

"I'm not exactly going to hide him." He looked at the sky, tracking a crow. "I'll explain when we get there. How much further by the way?"

"We're almost there."

Kristine said, "I hope Roosevelt isn't upset that we don't have any food this time." As if to amend this, she uprooted a chicory stalk, grown from the gravel. "We better bring him something." There were plenty of weeds along the way and she added sorrel and tall grass shoots to the bunch she carried. By the time they reached that place where the road dropped off into vacant lot, her arms were full.

For a moment, George was worried Roosevelt might be gone, that he might have wandered off in the night looking for Safeway. But as the city disappeared into leaves and trees, the smell of the lush ravine and sound of the creek, he knew where the elephant would be: right where they left him.

"Holy Mackerel!" Uncle Robert wheezed.

"Hi, Roosevelt," said Kristine, waving her bunches of flowers and weeds.

The elephant took a few steps towards them, waiting at the edge of the creek. Its reflection dappled and trembled with the movement of the stream then moved like a tow truck underwater reaching its trunk towards them.

Kristine hopped ahead of George and Uncle Robert balancing on a stone in the creek and holding up her arms.

With a chuff, Roosevelt gently took the bouquet, pulled it back across the shallow water and gulped it.

George joined Kristine on the flat rock. In a moment the trunk came back for the rest of the leaves. George patted it as it curled and coiled away.

"He sure is fond of you two," Uncle Robert said.

George turned around and asked his uncle, "What's going to happen to him?"

"I'm going to make him vanish from this place."

"How?" Both children stared at him. Kristine held to George for balance.

Uncle Robert tipped his top hat to rub his forehead. "It's something I first learned to do in dreams. Did you know, you actually have the power to change your dreams? All you need to do is be aware that you're in a dream. If something is happening you don't like, a nightmare or whatever, you simply make it different." He snapped his fingers. There was a moth hovering around him. "Actually, it took me years to make it work. But then I found out I could make it happen here too," he waved his hand around, "in this world… When I'm awake."

George and Kristine stared at him in such open-eyed wonder and expectation, the way two deer spotting you from the edge of the woods will do. Uncle Robert had to laugh. "Don't worry," he said. "Here's what I do…I picture Africa…The hundreds of miles of trees and yellow grasses…I feel myself going there… And I'm bringing Roosevelt with me…There's more elephants not far from us. Roosevelt sees them too and off he goes…" Uncle Robert opened his eyes. "Then I come back."

They all stood there silently thinking about it. They were people in a museum. There was the sound of the creek singing around the stones, birds perched on trees, and the low idle rumbling of the elephant.

"Okay," George said. "Let's try it."

"Don't you think you should tell Roosevelt good-bye first?"

"Oh," said George. He was glad his uncle thought of that. It would be terrible to think the elephant was suddenly gone.

Kristine waved.

"Goodbye, Roosevelt. And have a safe trip."

George stared at the elephant across the stream from him. It would be hard to believe Roosevelt was ever here at all. "Goodbye…"

They turned on their stone to face the man with the top hat.

Uncle Robert nodded. Then he shook the long sleeves of green sweater. He rolled his neck and stretched. Clearing his throat, he told them, "For this part I'm going to ask you to close your eyes. It's like doing a magic act, people shouldn't see how it's done."

George and Kristine closed their eyes and in that darkness listened to the water.

Roosevelt was gone. The space where he had been, in ferns, salal and huckleberry, seemed unbent by his disappearance…Nobody would ever guess looking at all that green that there had ever been an elephant there.

George slipped and put a foot in the shallow creek. The cold water crept right through his sock.

Kristine turned from the wooded hillside to face Uncle Robert. "You did it."

"Yeah," he sighed. "I—"

"What was that?!" a big voice came down from the top of the path. "Where's Roosevelt?!" Mel Tell's clown shoes tromped down the path towards the trio beside the stream. "I've never seen anything like it! Now you see it, now you don't." He stopped beside the quiet, tall Uncle Robert. "Only…Mister, I don't know how you did it?" Mel took a second to notice the boy and girl standing on a rock in the creek. "Hey!" he said, "You're that kid—George!"

"Yes. Hello, Mr. Tell."

Mel laughed. "Small world! I guess that elephant caller worked, huh?"

"Is that how you found this spot?" George took a big hop back to the soft sand.

"Listen," Mel confided. "When you've been with

an elephant as long as me, you know where they like to go. But now—" He shook his head admiringly at Uncle George and clucked, "That was pure magic." He let the heavy coil of rope slide off his shoulder. "Roosevelt's leash…I guess I won't be needing that…Unless you tell me where he went."

"East," Uncle Robert said. "Ten thousand miles or so."

"Yeah," said the clown. "That figures…I don't know how I'm going to explain this to the boss, though."

"I saw this book at school," George said. "It was about prehistoric animals and there was a picture of a wooly mammoth. It was stuck in a tar pit and sinking into the ground."

Mel tried it out, "Roosevelt sunk into the ground."

"That's what happened to Alice in Wonderland," Kristine said. "She went down to another world."

Mel corrected himself, "Roosevelt in Wonderland."

"Yes," Kristine said, liking the sound of it. "Like it happened in the book."

"Yeah, well, unfortunately this isn't a book." Mel Tell pointed at the green underbrush. "And in the circus' eyes, I just lost an elephant. I'm in big trouble." Then he thought of something. You could almost see the light bulb go on above his head. He put a hand on Robert's shoulder. "Unless you can make me disappear too!"

"Oh, no."

"No, this is a great idea!"

"No, I've never tried it with another person. There are too many things that could go wrong."

"Look—" Mel took a folded postcard from his coat pocket. He held it out for Robert to see. "Send me here…"

"Really?"

"Where is it?" Kristine and George leaned in to see the card.

Uncle Robert said, "Tahiti." It was a tinted blue sea, long white sandy beach and palm trees.

Mel beamed, "I've been waiting all my life to go there. Now's my chance!"

"No," Robert said. "I've never tried to move a person. People have too many ties and connections. Someone would come looking for you."

Mel shook his head. "All I have is the circus. And once they find out I lost an elephant, I won't even have that. Then where will I end up? A washed up ex-clown, holed up in some fleabag hotel, no prospects, no joy, no nothing."

"Ohhh," Kristine cried.

"Come on," Mel begged. "Send me to Tahiti."

"I shouldn't."

"You should," Mel said. "I've got nothing to lose and everything to gain."

Uncle Robert asked George, "What do you

think?"

George was looking at the postcard. It must have been carried in that pocket for years. The fold had been taped, the edges were worn, even the colors were faded from dreaming over.

Three people walked out of the gulley into the late afternoon. The hot daylight painted them in the field. All three of them—the boy, the girl, and the man in the top hat—took a moment to look back at the dark green where the creek rippled. The elephant and the circus clown were gone.

Uncle Robert handed the postcard to George. "I guess you can have this, if you'd like."

George took it.

"I needed to use it as a reference when I sent him," Uncle Robert explained.

George could almost feel the ocean breeze, hear it in the palms and the plash of the waves on the sand. It was beautiful, he thought, and no wonder the clown kept it always tucked away close to a beating heart.

George felt like climbing in there too. The beach looked like it went on forever. George held the picture closer. There was a tiny speck of a figure on that sand far away in the distance. He wondered if that was Mel Tell? Maybe the clown was living in this tinted photo now? Sometime that speck would come closer, become a silhouette with a suitcase and a coffee cup. Near enough to check on George, wave and wish him well and then go back into those sepia colors, into a Tahiti that existed out of sight.

The afternoon sun was starting to go down, sliding like a wet bead on a lemonade pitcher, when George and Uncle Robert said goodbye to Kristine at her door on Girard.

She waved, the screen door clacked shut and they walked on, only a couple more blocks to the house on Ellsworth.

George finally said it, "Why are you still here, living this way? Couldn't you send yourself anywhere in the world? Couldn't you picture a goldmine and scoop up an armful? Couldn't you also go where it's always sunny and peaceful?"

Uncle Robert let out a little puff of a laugh, enough to blow the dandelion seeds off a stalk. "I like it here, George." He touched a tall elm tree as they passed. "You know there's all kinds of wonders right here that you probably take for granted." He looked up at the tall tree canopy with all the other trees spread over the street. "I'm content."

"Oh," George said. "Well, I'd sure like to learn how to do that. I know there are places I'd like to go."

"I know." Uncle Robert put his hand on the boy's shoulder. "And you will."

Ellsworth was calm as a painting when they stepped foot on that chalked sidewalk leading to

George's house.

George thought of something else and quickly asked, "What if you thought about dinosaurs or King Arthur? Could you travel back in time?"

"Like H.G. Wells? Did you read that book of his I gave you?"

"Not yet…" George said.

"The Time Machine," Uncle Robert said dreamily. "You should read it. You'd like it. Hopping about in time is dangerous. What I did to that elephant and his keeper was just as risky. Who knows what they might do. You never know how things will be affected by what you do." He sighed. "If anything goes drastically wrong, I suppose I can rewind time and start over before the circus came to town."

"No! No, you can't, Uncle Robert. Too many things have happened that I wouldn't ever want to miss."

They stopped at the edge of George's yard. There were little blue flowers already coming up through the mown tracks from two days ago.

"Don't worry," he told George. "Just row, row, row your boat."

"What?"

Uncle Robert sang, "Merrily, merrily, merrily, merrily, life is but a dream."

George laughed and started across the grass.

"Oh," Uncle Robert remembered, "I'll be meeting you and Andrew later tonight. Andrew told me he wanted to see the city when the lights go out for the air raid."

"That's tonight?"

"Yes."

"Boy, what a busy day."

"It certainly is. And I still have an appointment to keep."

"What?" George asked.

"I need to find out what happens in my movie."

"That's right." Then George tuned in his radio voice again as he announced, "It will live in your memory forever."

Uncle Robert laughed and waved. "I'll see you later."

"Okay." But a moment later, George whirled his feet in the lawn. "Hey, Uncle Robert! Don't forget you have twins now!"

His uncle tipped his top hat back and bowed, extravagant as some long ago star of the stage. George paused and wondered where his uncle got such an old fashioned looking hat.

The radio was on and it had created a world. The Goldbergs were at the train station and you could see them there. Steam hissed in the air, travelers echoed on the platforms, coming and going to trains announced from speakers high on the marble pillars. And as their son, Sammy hurried off to his army troop train, Sammy Goldberg's mother comforted another, "Don't cry madam, your son…my son too. This is no time for crying. Today we have to stand like rocks in the sea. We all have to face the same way until our bodies become a wall that locks the fascists in their holes. Our sons go to the front, our husbands and our daughters make guns and tanks and bullets. And we will dry our eyes and stand like mountains. And when they're tired and weary we must be their strength. And when they're hurt we must be their health. And when the dark days come, and the dark days will come," Molly Goldberg's voice broke, "we must be their light. And in the end, in the end, madam, in victory we will have time to cry. We mothers should make a promise—we should swear to each other not to cry until the war is won."

The house was still as dust. George turned his head as the program ended and he could see his mother with her hand pushed to her face, covering her eyes.

George thought she might have been asleep.

During the commercial for Duz soap, George caught sight of Andrew appearing at the window. He waved for George to come outside.

The light was falling, it was like an ocean washing over. It was time to go to the harbor and see the whole city submerge.

Down Dupont Street they saw another one of those trucks with the megaphones. Actually, they heard it before they saw it. The amplified voice from it carried in the air for blocks, bouncing off fences and houses, reminding everyone of the air raid only an hour away. So much effort went into a war, even for one that wasn't here.

On either side of the sidewalk, they passed people who were pulling curtains tight over windows. Dark under the trees, the shadowy houses were covering their heads.

"Are you scared about tomorrow?" George asked. C Street gave them a view of the bay. They only had a few more streets to go. The mill made a thick cloud colored by the setting sun.

"Tomorrow I'll be out there." Andrew said simply.

George looked at the sparkling water and the islands breaking like whales. He guessed if he could see further—past the water on the other side, across the peninsula and snowy Olympic Mountains to where the Pacific Ocean broke on the shore—way over there in little tropical stepping stones lay the path to Japan. But he couldn't imagine his brother over there.

There weren't many people out walking and not only because the heat of the long July day still baked in the air. There was a feeling. Even the crows spreading out in skeins above, heading for their nesting trees knew there wasn't much time left before something was going to happen. They cawed back and forth, hurry up, hurry up, like ashes blown in the wind.

George watched the last pair of crows leave over the tin roof of the mill and said, "Andrew, do they have crows in Japan?"

"I think so."

"And in Germany?"

"I suppose."

That made George think of something. We all have crows in all our cities and towns…He wanted to say something about that but expressing what it meant was just out of his reach.

"Come on, George." Andrew was stopped on the steep ramp going down to the dark. Tied to it, sitting in the water, was their blue sailboat.

"Hey!" George cried out. He nearly bounced down the ramp. "You fixed her up! Are we going out?" The sun had set but the bay looked peaceful in the purple dusk.

"No," Andrew said. "We're not. I am."

"But you're not allowed to. The scout manual says you can't go out alone in a boat, especially at night. And we don't have any running lights either."

"George. Where I'm going I don't want to be seen. I'm not going on that train tomorrow. I'm sailing to that island instead." He pointed at the silhouette of dark fir trees laying like a sleeping cow. "I'm going to live there until the war blows over."

"What? Where?"

Andrew smiled. "You remember that time we went there? You were playing explorer. We went into those woods and we kept walking past where the path ended and we found that apple orchard in the middle of all those fir trees and there was that old farm house. Everything was overgrown but that house was just like somebody left it."

George listened, nodded.

"That's where I'll be staying. I have my supplies in the boat, and I'll live on apples like Johnny Apple-seed."

"Well," George stammered. "The milkman says the wars won't ever stop."

"I'm only worried about this war," Andrew said. "I'll come back when it's over." He put his arms around his brother and gave him a strong hug.

George tried not to let go. He didn't want to, but as his brother released him, George was starting to cry. He tried to fight those big tears welling in his eyes, he felt like a candle tipping out wax.

Andrew stepped into the sailboat. He was doing something with the ropes and George had to wipe his eyes to see.

Andrew untied the lines holding the boat to the dock.

"I don't want you to go," George managed to say.

"I know. We'll be okay though. You know, some

night I'll have to sneak back here and check on you and Mom and Dad. You'll see me at the window, real quiet." He cast off from land. "Don't say a word about where I've gone." He turned his back to George; he needed to use both hands to hoist the sail. It was getting so dark he was turning into shadow.

George stood in the dark and watched the boat leave. All the lights were turned off and for a moment the city was beautiful, mysterious, the pulp mill was as ancient looking as a fairy tale castle. The stars popped out like flowers. George raised his arm to wave and say something but his voice was lost in the air raid.

From the very top of the Puget Sound Pulp and Timber plant, the air raid siren groaned into life and rose in tone to a splitting shriek so loud George had to cover his ears. The dots of light in windows, on towers and streetlamps and even the red neon *Herald* sign went dark. The siren unwound then started up again. For three minutes it continued to scream, over and over joining the chorus overseas that walked the living into dying, day after day, night after night. For three long minutes it made a war where there wasn't one.

George lay flat on the dock with his eyes closed, breathing through his nose the smell of the sea imprinted in the wood, trying again to make himself invisible.

Why did he think coming to the waterfront tonight would be something to see? Maybe this was why, he thought—all alone and terrified and the city screaming like a tortured monster—now he knew what it was like in Berlin or London, Tokyo, or anywhere the bombs were falling.

Finally, the siren gave a long sustained all-clear blast, and the hot steam moaned clear of its hollow works.

The ringing silence stung in George's ears. Sitting up, he felt the tremors in him like a tuning fork vibrating instead of flesh and bone, like he was a boy made of shallow creek water radiating. He could sink back into the sea.

He saw the lights begin to come back on. They flicked on everywhere, the city was coming back, it hadn't been bombed out. Tall buildings that would have been rubble stood instead, filled with light.

George turned from them to search the bay. The boat was gone, no sign of that little white sail. His brother was gone. The darkness seemed all consuming.

With his head so full of ringing, George hadn't heard his name being called. George didn't even know his uncle stood at the top of the ramp until he started to descend and the shaking reached George's dock.

"Uncle Robert!"

His uncle said something but no words came from him, only the shadows on his face moved.

George rubbed his ears. All the sound in the world had been turned off. "Uncle Robert," he said, forming what he hoped could be heard. "I can't hear!"

The lights on the pulp mill reflected on the water and faintly on his uncle.

"I don't know what you're saying!" George panicked. "I can't hear!"

Uncle Robert touched his lips. He made the O-K sign with his hand. He touched his wrist, his watch and spun his finger. "Wait..." he said slowly, so the word could be read. He tapped his ear. "Wait a while. You will hear." He smiled and hugged George. The boy looked so scared.

When Uncle Robert let go and looked at George again, his nephew looked better. A streetlight had gone on up above, glowing on a post. Soon there would be moths circling it again.

"You want to go home?" Uncle Robert asked in big, slow words.

George understood. 1942, like a ship in a bottle, sails up, sealed up, was stuck in time. He thought about what Uncle Robert said to do with your nightmares and replacing realities. George and Kristine had seen it happen. Mel Tell went to Tahiti and Roosevelt…with practice you could make an elephant disappear. He nodded. The dark world had gone quiet. And things that disappear in the dark…his brother, his hearing…would come back, wouldn't they? George had to think so. It was time to go. Like a crow holding out a wing, he reached for and took that big hand.

Quotations from:

The Bellingham Herald, 'Model Airplane Contest Planned,' 7/19/1942.

The Green Hornet radio program: 'A Slip of the Lip,' broadcast, 5/30/1942.

The Thin Man radio program 'The Strange Case of Professor Wainger,' broadcast 1942.

Moontide, 20th Century Fox, opened in Bellingham in July, 1942.

The Goldbergs radio program 'Sammy Goes Away to Army,' broadcast 7/23/1942.

Other Books by the Author

Ohio Trio (Bottom Dog Press 2001)
Bowl of Water (Bottom Dog Press 2003)
Another Life (Bird Dog Publishing 2007)
Home Recordings (Bird Dog Publishing 2009)
The Mermaid Translation (Bird Dog Publishing 2010)
The Selected Correspondence of Kenneth Patchen
    edited by Allen Frost (Bottom Dog Press 2012)
The Wonderful Stupid Man (Bird Dog Publishing 2012)
Saint Lemonade (Good Deed Rain 2014)
Playground (Good Deed Rain 2014)

CPSIA information can be obtained at www.ICGtesting.com
Printed in the USA
BVOW07s1812040215

386395BV00002B/25/P